Helicopter Man Pounds Dinosaur Billionaire Ass

CHUCK TINGLE

ISBN: 1517103150
ISBN-13: 978-1517103156

All handsome men remove their skin after work; keeps it nice and tight. Maybe one day I can remove my skin and be a handsome man, too. Hope so.

- Chuck Tingle

CONTENTS

ACKNOWLEDGMENTS

Thank you to my friend, Hunter. You are my best friend and the soul of books, you made love real for all buds who do guy stuff.

No thanks to the joker man, Ted Cobbler.

1 MY NAME IS JOHN HAMS

"My name is John Hams and I'm a sex addict." I say, a mantra that I know like the back of my hand by now.

I look down at the literal back of my hand for a moment and study myself. Sometimes I feel like a stranger in my own skin, and tonight is one of those nights. How the hell did I even end up here?

"Hi John!" The crowd responds with a resounding chorus of support.

I've been coming to these meetings for a long time, and this part is still difficult. Once I start talking the words will just flow out of my brain and into the air like beautiful confessional butterflies, but for the first few seconds of silence between my greeting and their response, it feels like I'm sitting atop a giant roller coaster just waiting for the plunge. The butterflies remain firmly planted within the pit of my stomach. The hair on the back of my neck stands straight up as I try desperately to will myself into speaking.

Finally, my lips part and my story comes tumbling out.

"It's been two years since my last sexual encounter with a billionaire dinosaur." I tell the group, a ragtag bunch of fellow addicts sitting around in the loose formation of a circle.

We're in the dimly lit corner of a church basement at the far end of Hollywood boulevard, past the glitz and the glamour, where the liquor stores start to pop up and the gleeful tourists fade away. The only ones left to wander around over here are down and out actors and failed screenwriters, angst filled shells of their former selves who swear up and down that they could've been the one if they'd only landed that role.

1

Maybe next time, they think.

The group responds to my admission with a smatter of supportive congratulations. I nod in appreciation, accepting one of the few things in my life right now that I can truly be proud of, my abstinence.

"Honestly, I don't really think about billionaire dinosaur sex all that much anymore." I tell the group. "It's gotten to the point where it just doesn't seem to cross my mind, and I'm working all the time so that makes things a little easier." I laugh. "Work is a fucking pain these days."

"What's hard about work?" Our group leader, Forbok asks.

Forbok is a handsome older man, who was once a porn star in the golden age of VHS tapes and late night, adult channel skin flicks. You can still see it in the way that he carries himself, with the confidence and knowledge that, at one point, he could have had any man, woman or prehistoric beast that he wanted just by flashing a smile and giving a sly little wink.

Apparently, the industry wasn't all that good to Forbok in his later years, because he ended up here with the rest of us, having abstained from his own billionaire dinosaur vice for nearly a decade. Forbok says that he's saving himself until he finds the one, a perfect, wealthy Tyrannosaurs Rex who can somehow undo all of the trauma and anxiety that has mummified his sex life, but I have my doubts. Straight up, I don't think Forbok ever wants to see another prehistoric penis again.

"Work is..." I trail off. "Work. I mean, nobody really likes to work do they?"

"Some of us do." Forbok tells me. "This is what I do for work and I love it."

"True." I say, nodding, "But, you of all people know what it's like to take it up the ass for a paycheck."

A heavy, and achingly awkward, silence falls over the room.

The second that the words left my mouth I had regretted them. I wasn't trying to be mean in any way, not at all, but there is a certain sting to my joke that I can't help notice now that it's all too late.

Full disclosure, in some ways, I'm a little jealous of Forbok. We're both brothers in Jurassic billionaire abstinence, but every day I'm growing more and more convinced that I don't really have a choice in the matter. Even if I wanted a hot raptor in my life, I'm not sure that I could find one. Forbok, on the other hand, is still a stunner and, in his mid forties, he's almost twice my age.

Don't get me wrong, I'm not terrible looking by any stretch, but there are certainly no delusions of a male modeling carrier in my future. Average weight and a little on the short side, with mousy brown hair and a face that I'm not entirely happy with. I'm just another face in the crowd, and I've come to terms with that.

Forbok, on the other hand, could still probably steal the brontosaurus boyfriend off of any hot little twink that strutted his way in here if he really wanted to. Luckily, the guy knows a thing or two about restraint, and he's also got a sense of humor.

"You're right about that!" Forbok finally says, laughing at my joke and signaling to the rest of the group that it's okay to join in at his expense. God damn, I love this guy; so solid in his own self worth. In the entire time that I've been coming to this Hollywood meeting, I've never seen him lose his cool.

"I don't know what it is that makes work so awful these days." I blurt, collecting my thoughts again and trying to focus. "It kind of sucks to that the raptors at the lab see me as such a ... prude, I guess."

I glance around the circle of fellow billionaire dinosaur sex addicts, looking for any kind of response but only met with their steady gazes. One of two of the men nod in understanding, which is all the encouragement that I need.

"They know I'm not seeing anyone." I continue. "But they've all tried to hook up with me and I've stayed strong. Now that the option isn't there any longer it's like I'm invisible. Meanwhile there's this new guy, Donald, who I just know is already fucking his way to the top. He's been at the lab a quarter of the time that I've been there and already received two promotions. One more and he's technically going to be my boss."

A stegosaurus sitting directly across from me in the circle raises his hand and I nod in his direction. I've never seen him before, but the second that our eyes meet I can feel something strange blossom inside of me, a tiny pin prick of my heart that floods out across my veins like a warm, pleasant ache.

This is why we shouldn't have interspecies sexaholics meetings, I think to myself. Apparently, in the officially sanctioned groups, they split things up between humans, dinosaurs, unicorns and bigfeet as a steadfast and unbreakable rule, but our wild bunch is technically not an official chapter of

Sexaholics Anonymous, just Forbok's personal bit of community service. He uses a lot of the same methods of the bigger meeting groups, to the point where many of our members are supplementing there official meetings by coming here on the side, but we're still not the real deal.

Besides, even if this guys a handsome dinosaur, it doesn't automatically mean that he's a handsome billionaire dinosaur. That's a stereotype I've made leaps and bounds towards eliminating from my brain. We've had all types of creatures come and go from these meetings and it's never been a problem. At least, not yet.

"I'm sorry, I think I must have missed it. Where do you work?" The stegosaurus asks with genuine curiosity. "Most people say office, you say lab."

Forbok immediately steps in. "Actually, John Hams has a government job that is very strict about its secrecy. We're all about being open here but, as we've covered before, this is something that we're not going to talk about."

The dinosaur lowers his beautiful blue eyes, looking somewhat ashamed of himself.

"It's okay." I tell him. "I just can't really talk about it."

There is an strange silence as the entire room looks inward, everyone running wild with their own personal suspicions of what I could possibly be doing out at Buttcorp laboratories.

Eventually, Forbok claps his hands together in an attempt to get things moving again.

"Anything else you'd like to talk about tonight?" He asks me.

I shake my head. "Nah, that's about it."

"Thanks for sharing." Forbok says, which is everyone else's cue to burst into a solid applause. "Peter, you're up next."

Peter, the older man sitting next to me, starts to speak loudly about his craving for gay jet planes but I tune him out, instead focusing on the handsome, dinosaur newcomer directly across the way.

There is something utterly intoxicating about the guy's presence, a strange mixture of confidence and intelligence that I can't quite put my finger on. He's laid back and unassuming, as if he doesn't need to be the loudest, biggest retile in the room simply because he already knows that he is.

Basically, he seems like the opposite of every dinosaur that I've ever gone for; cool and controlled.

After the meeting is finished, I head over to the snack table and start filling up on chips and dip. I've been so unhappy at work lately that I've started avoiding going home following functions like this, because I know that the next step is sleep and then comes the morning and another long workday at the lab. Oh, the life of a single, celibate man.

I make my way down the table; picking at some hummus and pita, followed by a few baby carrots and then a chocolate chip cookie.

"Hey." Comes a warm voice from behind me.

I spin around abruptly and come face to face with the handsome stegosaurus newcomer.

"I'm Yorb Killcorn." He says, extending his hand. "I just wanted to apologize for earlier, I didn't know that questions about your job were off limits, I was just trying to be proactive. I'm new here."

"John Hams." I tell him, reaching out and giving Yorb a friendly handshake.

Now that I'm this close to him, I can finally discern just how handsome this creature actually is. Yorb is perfectly chiseled in every way, from his jaw line down to the hint of scaly muscular chest that peeks out from the edge of his heather gray v-neck. The spines that line their way across his back are, frankly, breathtaking.

I can feel a slight throbbing ache deep within my loins, a place that literally hasn't been touched in years. I already know that talking to this guy is probably a bad idea, (After all, what better why to relapse than with a fellow addict?) but I can't help being slowly charmed by his quietly confident demeanor. Thank god he's not a billionaire.

But then again, what's a little harmless flirting?

"Yeah, Forbok was a little harsh on you about that." I tell Yorb, glancing over at the man in question as he holds the door for a few exiting members with a smile and a nod. "He means well though."

"Yeah." Yorb agrees. "I can see that, he seems really great. I think I could get a lot of good out of this place."

I eye him curiously. There's more to this stegosaurs than meets the eye, that's for sure.

"You didn't share today." I tell him, as if he hadn't noticed.

"Nah, not yet." Yorb explains. "Didn't seem like the right time, first meeting and all."

I shrug. "Whatever, it takes some people months of listening before they open up."

The two of us stand here for a moment and I'm not exactly sure what to say next. Yorb doesn't seem to mind though, perfectly comfortable with the silence.

"Do you want to go grab something to eat?" Yorb finally asks.

I want so badly to say yes but, the second his words hit my ears, alarm bells start ringing deep within my brain. I can't even remember the last time I was asked out by a dinosaur that was this handsome, rich or poor. By all accounts, Yorb seems like the full package that any reasonable man would be swooning after.

I start to open my mouth and then hesitate, catching the words in my throat. I quickly change course.

"I don't think that's a good idea." I tell him.

I fully expect Yorb to be devastated by the news, but instead he smiles warmly. "No worries."

His confidence unwavering, Yorb turns his attention back to the table of food, where he grabs a slice of ham and then takes a bite. He chews slowly and swallows, then quickly washes it down with a shot of chocolate milk.

"I'm sorry." I say, immediately regretting my decision to turn him down, and his lack of disappointment only making things even worse for me.

Yorb shrugs. "You seem like a very nice guy but, honestly, I get it. This is the last place I should be trying to get a date."

I don't say anything because he's right, but I don't care. I want nothing more than for the two of us to get out of here and grab a drink, to talk to each other like neither of us are the damaged addicts that we are. I miss the mystery and suspense of being around a secure, sexy dinosaur.

"Well, it was nice to meet you, John Hams." Yorb says, giving me a little wink. "I'll see you at the next meeting."

With that, Yorb turns and heads towards the door, leaving me in a state of speechless yearning. I watch as he exchanges a few words with Forbok and then departs into the warm Hollywood night, flipping a small silver coin into the air and then catching it again with his hand.

It's one thing to refrain from billionaire dinosaur sex, but did I really have to deny every creature connection that comes my way?

I let out a long sigh and gather my things, heading home alone once again.

2 BUTTCORP

I swipe my keycard and wait for the Buttcorp front door to unlock.

Nothing happens.

I swipe it again, this time drifting the thin, plastic rectangle even slower over its glowing card reader.

Still no recognition from the machine as I glance down at my watch and see that today's big meeting starts in just five minutes. I look over my shoulder to see if anyone else is around who might be able to let me in, but it appears that everyone else is already inside and waiting for the meeting to begin.

"Fuck." I mutter out loud, pounding on the door with my fist and then cupping my hands around my eyes as I peer through the dark glass for any sign of like. "Hello? My keycard isn't working for some reason!"

There's no response.

I know for a fact that there's a back entrance to our lab facility, all the way on the other side of the building, but that one is well out of the way and almost certainly locked up tight.

The projects that we work on here at Buttcorp are incredibly powerful and often dangerous, so I'm not in favor of lighter security, but at least get some security that works.

Suddenly, the glass panel door next to me pops open and Tucker, our front gate security officer, pokes his head out.

"Thank you so much!" I tell him, trying to rush past.

Tucker puts his hand up and stops me.

"Excuse me." He says, sternly. "This is a high security laboratory, I'm gonna need to see some identification."

I can't help but give me a strange look, unsure of whether or not the man is joking. I've said hello to him almost every morning for the past two years and suddenly he has no idea who I am.

"Are you kidding me?" I ask. "It's John Hams."

Tucker shakes his head. "Sir, I'm gonna need to see some identification."

I stare at him for a minute longer, flabbergasted, then finally hand him my keycard.

Tucker looks at the plastic rectangle for a moment and then flips it over.

"There's no photo on this." Tucker tells me. He reaches over and runs it across the scanner. Predictably, nothing happens.

"Tucker!" I shout. "Are you kidding me?"

"No keycard, no entry." He says.

"My keycard is broken!" I yell, losing it a little.

Being late for the meeting is one thing, but now my lack of respect around this office is really getting to me. How could I have been so forgettable to this man?

Suddenly, Tuckers eyes light up as he glances past me. "Oh! Good morning, Donald!" He calls.

I look over my shoulder to see Donald Trumbs, the handsome, redheaded new guy who's everyone's favorite around the lab, walking up the path behind me. Tucker immediately holds the door open for him and steps back so that the hunky dude can enter.

"John?" He asks, surprised to see me. "What the fuck are you doing out here? The meeting's in like two minutes and we're gonna be late."

"I'm trying to get inside but I can't!" I cry, throwing my hands up in the air. "My keycard's messed up!"

Donald Trumbs flies through the door and I try to follow behind but Tucker stops me once again, stepping in front of me and shaking his head with authority.

"Seriously?" I yell.

Donald turns around and quickly assesses the situation. "Oh, he's fine Tucker. Let him through."

Turker glances back at Donald, and then nods and allows me to pass without a hint of hesitation. "Good god, thank you." I gasp in frustration, and then struggle to catch up to the heartthrob as he barrels ahead through a series of long, sterile hallways.

"You didn't get the email about picking up your new keycard?" Donald Trumbs asks. "The whole security system's been revamped from the ground up."

I'm almost positive that I didn't get an email, but just to make sure I pull out my phone as we walk and open up my mailbox. There are no messages saying anything about a new security system.

"I didn't get anything." I tell him.

Donald shrugs. "Maybe they forgot to send it to you? I don't know."

As if I didn't already feel invisible enough in this crowd of scientists, now I'm not even on the official laboratory mailing list.

I put my phone back into my pocket and almost immediately Donald and I arrive at the conference room of our meeting, which has already started. Donald pushes through the door and I follow behind, immediately halting the voice of our T-Rex boss, Doctor Cobbler, who stands before a giant, oblong table full of other scientists and lab technicians.

Everyone simultaneously turns to look at us as we head to either side of the table and quietly slip into the only two empty seats left.

"John Hams." Doctor Cobbler nods. "Donald, so glad you could make it."

"I'm sorry, Doctor." Donald says. "I just lost track of time this morning, it won't happen again."

Doctor Cobbler gives him an accepting smile of sharp, bladelike teeth, something that I completely did not expect. Cobbler is the definition of a hard ass dinosaur, especially when it comes to being punctual. I look back and forth between the two of them as it slowly dawns on me that they are probably fucking.

I try my best to stay calm, but it's a real struggle to maintain my mood against the tide of anger and frustration that washes over me.

Doctor Cobbler turns his attention to me now. "And you, John Hams? What's your excuse?"

I sit up in my chair almost immediately, trying to look as professional as possible. "My keycard isn't working for some reason. I was standing right outside the front door forever this morning trying to get in."

Doctor Cobbler's eyes brim with annoyance and disappointment. "You didn't read the email about security being updated around here?

Project Handsome Helicopter is at an incredibly important phase, we need to step everything up at this point."

"I know." I tell him, desperately trying to explain. "It's not that I didn't read the email, I didn't even get it."

Doctor Cobbler sighs loudly through his large dinosaur snout.

I can't help but notice some of the other scientist around the table exchanging quick glances, reveling in the fact that I'm about to be taken to task by our boss.

"Just…" Doctor Cobbler starts, clearly upset. He pauses for a moment and then tries again. "I'm sorry. We're all under a lot of stress right now, myself included. Just go see Hank in lab seventeen, he'll set up with a new keycard."

"Thank you." I say with a nod, then stand up and quickly exit the conference room.

As the door closes behind me I can't help but hear Donald add. "Well, *I* got the email!"

I start making my way deeper into the facility, seething, but trying my best to hurry back for the rest of the meeting. Time to suck it up, I tell myself. This has become my daily mantra.

The farther I get, however, the more my frustration evolves into a genuine lack of care. I feel like I am up against a wall and, at this point, any more effort from my end is just going to go to waist. As the token frumpy, celibate guy who won't bang billionaire dinosaurs around here, I could probably show back up in the conference room a week from now and people would barely notice.

By now, my pace has evolved into what could only be described as a mosey; sauntering down the halls and peering into the windows of various laboratories that are well beyond my clearance level. I've still got a lot of area to cover before I reach lab seventeen, so I might as well see if I can scope out something interesting while I'm at it.

I suddenly realize that this is the emptiest I've seen the lab here since I started working at Buttcorp; all of the head scientists in conference with Doctor Cobbler while the lower level technicians are at home for the day, waiting for the new security protocols to be implemented. The whole time that I've been walking, I haven't run across a single other living soul.

Having not seen the most recent developments in Project Handsome Helicopter for myself, all of this precaution seems a little unnecessary, but I suppose that if it's anything like they say it is, we have reason to be fearful.

Project Handsome Helicopter is the first stage of a technology that Buttcorp has been contracted to develop for the United States military, specifically the Special Operations Taskforce. It's not the first work we've done for the military, but it's certainly the most secretive and well guarded; with all of our employees signing gag orders almost immediately after locking down the official bid for the job.

The basic premise of this project is a practical application of the nanotechnogly that I helped create here at Buttcorp when I first arrived two years ago.

For those you don't spend your lives buried in thick computer science textbooks, Nanotechnology is an exciting, and frankly horrifying, new field of robotics.

It's simple enough. Take a robot and make it smaller, then smaller, and then smaller still; until the robot itself is the size of a cell.

We are all made of building blocks that are fused together in just the right way to create the shape of a human being, billions upon billions of atoms stacked in a pile that can eventually walk and talk and grow. Some people find this method of looking at the universe as sad and lonely, breaking everything down to a scale that's so analytical and scientific that it leaves no room for those incredible moments of magic that life is all about.

I, on the other hand, think that this is where the magic truly lies, right down here at the base level of all existence. It's why I became a computer scientist in the first place.

Once you have robots this small, there is no telling what you can do. Stack enough cell sized nanobots in the right arrangement and you've got yourself a bowl of ice cream, with absolutely no difference in taste or sensation when compared to the real thing. Even living creatures are made up of cells that can be replicated with nanobot programming; a tiny insect, a playful dog, or even a human being. Most importantly, we are creating the ability for any normal man to transform himself into a handsome helicopter with great abs and a killer smile.

When people talk about scientists going too far and playing god, this is exactly the type of thing they are talking about. It's a dangerous game, but if we don't harness this technology then someone else will.

Project Handsome Helicopter is Buttcorp's first attempt at combining nanobots with a human's natural biology, allowing the tiny machines to fuse with the cellular structure of a willing host through the means of a simple injection. Once this is done, the applications are endless, but we are starting simple enough.

Our first goal is to program our nanobots with the ability to change a person's physical appearance at will.

Essentially, we're on the verge of creating real world helicopter shape shifting. Hell, with enough scientific progress and long hours at the lab, we could eventually start turning people into cute jet planes.

The process is still a long ways off for human beings, but we've tested it on rats and already received astonishing results. In one study, the rodents were put into a tank with a portion of food located on the other side of a clear glass panel. Rats certainly can't fly, but they can after turning themselves into tiny little helicopters.

After their injection, however, It only took ten minutes for the rats to shift into very, very attractive helicopters and fly up over the tank's divider.

It was incredible to watch, and had I not seen it with my own eyes, I wouldn't have believed in a million years that this kind of technology was even possible.

Of course, all of the rats died only hours later, their bodies eventually changing into shapes not meant to support biological life. We've tried everything that we could to revise our nanobot code into a stable program, but all of the trails have been failures.

At this point we've narrowed the programming down into four distinct nanobot codes; but without more testing, we're not quite sure which one is going to remain stable, if any.

I finally reach laboratory seventeen and try swiping my keycard, only to find that the entire card scanner doesn't exist. Instead, there is a gaping hole where the machine used to be, the lock left wide open. I must have arrived here at the precise moment of transformation, the building itself changing right before my very eyes as we upgrade security systems.

I slowly push the door to the lab open and peer into the darkness. The overhead lights are off but the room is abuzz with all sorts of flickering displays, running at full speed in the dark as they process data. I've never been in here before, so I'm not sure what to expect, but I'm damn near positive that this isn't the right place for me to receive my new keycard.

"Hello?" I call out into the void, stepping through the threshold of the doorway. There has definitely been a mistake, and I realize almost immediately that, in his rush, Doctor Cobbler had told me to go to lab seventeen instead of lab seven. This room was way beyond my security clearance.

The second that I realize my mistake I hear footsteps approaching down the long hallway behind me, and my heart skips a beat. I'm already on thin ice as it is and, based on my experience in the conference room this morning, I have no doubt that Doctor Cobbler will have little patience to hear out my explanation for being in a restricted area, even if it's his own damn fault.

If there's one thing powerful dinosaurs hate doing, it's admitting that they were wrong.

With only a few seconds to spare, I decide to duck back into the darkness, hiding away under what I assume is a large desk. I try to remain as silent as possible.

From here I can see two figures talking briefly in the hallway. Soon, they get back to work installing the laboratory door's new card reader.

I try my best to breathe quietly, scooting as far back into the corner as I can while the two unassuming men work on their installation.

"Did you see what was in that last room?" One of the guys asks, his voice trembling.

"We're not here to judge." Says his coworker, solemnly.

"Those poor little mice, they were all stretched out and..." the man trails off, clearly upset. "Warped. I don't' know. They were spinning around the tank like little broken helicopters."

"They were rats." Says the man. "Not mice."

"I don't give a fuck what they were." The first guy replies. "They were living things." Suddenly, he bursts into a fit of tears, unable to control himself.

"Jumbi!" The man shouts. "You need to get a hold of yourself! We've got a job to do!"

Jumbi can barely speak through the tears. "I install fucking security systems, Dan! I didn't sign up to work for some mad scientist."

The two of them fight for a while, with Dan struggling to keep Jumbi together while he throws professionalism out the window for the sake of a few rat corpses.

To be fair, though, when the experiments don't go as planned and the nanobot programs become corrupted, the results can be pretty horrific.

I've gotten used to it at this point, but for someone who's never seen such a thing I'm not all that surprised by his reaction.

Eventually, Jumbi loses control completely and devolves into a blubbering mess, sobbing uncontrollably.

"Alright, you need to go." Dan finally says. "You can't come in here and lose it like this over someone else's job!"

"I know! I know!" Jumbi repeats. "I'm sorry."

Dan lets out a long sigh. "Okay, just... you need to get out of here. Why don't you head home for the day?"

Jumbi stops for a moment, sniffling loudly. It would appear that he likes this idea. "You sure?" He asks.

"Yeah, just don't let them see you crying on the way out." Dan says.

Through a small window in the door, I can see Jumbi's silhouette stand up and wipe the tears away from his eyes.

Jumbi seems young and slightly too fragile to be spending his time in a place like this.

"I'm a mess." Jumbi moans. "They're gonna see me like this."

Dan tosses him his jacket. "Just put that over your head and head straight for the door. I don't care if it looks weird, I don't want anyone to see that you've been crying. They hired us knowing that you were a helicopter and I had to convince them that you could handle it. My ass is on the line here, got that? Be professional."

"Got it." Jumbi confirms. "I'm sorry, boss."

"Good." Dan says. "Now get out of here, fly straight home."

The teary eyed man leaves quickly as Dan continues to work on the door's new security panel. I get the feeling that these two wouldn't have cared about finding me in here, or wouldn't have even known that I shouldn't be hanging around. Now that I've been hiding in the dark for a while, though, coming out and surprising him just seems incredibly creepy and weird.

It doesn't take long for Dan to finish working though, and just as quickly as he began the man is gone once more, moving off down the hall towards the next installation on his list.

I let out a long sigh of relief and begin to climb out from under wherever I've found myself hidden beneath, but my movement is abruptly stopped when I accidentally kick a long metal beam and hear a deafening metallic slam from all around me.

Immediately, my entire field of vision is assaulted with blinding white light, and I quickly realize that I'm now trapped within some just of large, coffin-like metallic box. My brain in a complete panic, I start pounding my firsts against the walls, screaming as loud as I can for someone to rescue me from this strange contraption. Seconds later, the box begins to fill with a bizarre, sweet smelling smoke, which causes me to choke and cough wildly.

I have no idea what I'm inhaling, but the fear that comes along with this foreign invasion of my body kicks my panic into overdrive, clawing at the walls of my airtight chamber with more ferocity than I've ever known.

"Help!" I scream, trying now to kick out the floor below me. "I'm trapped!"

Suddenly, a low hum starts to shake the entire chamber, rumbling up through my body and vibrating me faster and faster until my eyes hurt and my teeth chatter loudly. The bright white light shifts into a strange green hue and then begins to flicker, completely disorienting me and causing me to let out a sickly moan.

My entire body feels blazing hot now, as if I've suddenly been hit with a powerful fever. It tingles and burns across my entirety, spreading from the top of my head all the way down to my feet as I contort spastically with discomfort. I feel as though my skin is painfully expanding and contracting with every breath that I take, the heat growing and growing until finally it shifts into a pleasant numbness.

3 THESE BLADES ARE MADE FOR FLYING

Moments later, the vibration below me slows and soon enough I find myself whole again, the lights within the chamber flickering off and the lid above me popping open with a loud hiss.

I crawl out into the darkness coughing, trying to collect my bearings on the lab floor.

It takes a while, but eventually I'm able to climb to my feet and stagger over to the room's main light switch, which I flick on immediately and then spin around.

What I see makes me gasp in astonishment.

There before me is a stack of four strange chambers, inlaid into the back wall of the lab from floor to ceiling and surrounded by a plethora of strange, scientific equipment.

It takes me a moment to put everything together, but the second that I see the familiar nanobots containment system, I know exactly what this is. Buttcorp has been secretly developing an airborne delivery system for the Project Handsome Helicopter, and each chamber represents a different version of the code.

Even more terrifying, though, is the realization that I've now been exposed.

Suddenly, I feel as though the floor is falling out from under me. I grab onto the wall and try to stable myself, reeling from the news that my very existence could be snuffed out any second from now.

The nanobot code is still incredibly unstable. Not only could these be my very last breaths of life, but there is a very, very good chance that they will be.

However, I'm smart enough to understand that, at this point, any amount of panicking will only add to the instability of the program, and looking down at my hand I can already see the results of this hypothesis. My fingers have started to jut off in strange directions, contorting and pulling themselves together like the blade of a helicopter. It's not painful, really, but it certainly is terrifying, especially because I know what will happen if the program becomes too unstable.

"Oh fuck, oh fuck." I start to mutter to myself, holding my hand up to my face as it slowly becomes flatter and flatter. "Stay calm, John. Get it together."

The word 'calm' comes out all slurred and weird, and I glance down to see that part of my lip is drifting out away from my body, becoming translucent like the front window of an aircraft.

Suddenly, my thoughts jump to all of the mental work I've put in throughout the years with my meetings. The way that I've managed to master my thoughts and feelings, cultivating a system of tranquility that has kept me stable and sane, without a single relapse. I may be literally falling apart, but my mind is trained and stable as a rock.

Instead of screaming out in fear, I remain silent and I turn my thoughts inward, focusing on my breathing as I attempt to lower my heart rate.

Shockingly, it works, and before I know it my fingers are slowly but surely returning to their original form. The program is stabilizing.

Once everything is back where it belongs, I breathe out a thankful sigh of relief. The code now imbedded within my cells could, and probably will, still corrupt over time, but at least that time is not right now.

Quickly collecting myself, both literally and figuratively, I turn around and try to open the laboratory door, finding it to be firmly locked from both the inside and the out. Without a new keycard there's no hope for me, and even if I did have one I still wouldn't possess the security clearance to get in here. In other words, I'm fucked.

Of course, someone will eventually come by and find me in here, but what happens then? Best-case scenario, they will see that the forth chamber has been triggered and I'll be quarantined indefinitely (They can do this, I've read the fine print in my employment contract top to bottom). I don't even want to think about the worst-case scenario, especially now that the

United States government is involved.

Flashes of tiny, cold isolation cells and military tribunals flash through my head. Sure, I still have my rights, but now that the nanobots have completely fused with the structure of my body, I'm technically a piece of Buttcorp, and government, property. They have every right to do with me whatever they want.

I'll admit it, maybe I'm just being paranoid about the whole thing. But I'd rather not have to find out the hard way.

I have to get out of here.

Suddenly, it feels as if a switch has been flipped in my brain and I go into full-on problem solver mode. I'm focused and sharp, scanning my surroundings for anything that could help me escape this lab before someone returns. The meeting should be ending any moment now, giving me very little time to make my move.

Using the keypad is a dead end, encrypted well beyond anything I could hope to decipher even if I had my laptop handy. The door itself is made of solid steel and it's not going anywhere.

My gaze finally stops at the bottom of the door, focusing on the crack between it's solid metal face and the floor below. There's not even close to enough room for an arm to slip under it, but certainly enough for a helicopter blade.

I close my eyes and try my best to focus on the rhythm of my body, the way that it feels to simply exist within my own shell. I take it all in; the sensation of my lungs expanding and contracting, my heart thumping, my veins pushing blood throughout my entire being.

Once I've done this, I turn my attention to the molecules of my neck and arms, trying to imagine them stretching and pulling apart like taffy, transforming into the body of a handsome helicopter. It's not long before the internal sensation of myself starts to shift. I open my eyes and find that I'm extending towards door crack, my arm elongating itself in a strange but beautiful arc that quickly evolves into a flattened blade.

To my surprise, my clothes stretch around me, as well, somehow infused with the same nanobots that make up my biology. Everything that was locked inside that chamber with me is now one, single entity.

Soon, I find my arm slipping under the door and then drifting upwards towards the outside handle. I tug on it and, as I suspected, with the new keycard system I am still stuck, regardless of which side I try to open the door from. There's only one option left.

In one swift movement I swipe my helicopter blade from left to right, chopping the lock off and letting it clatter down onto the floor below. The door creaks slowly open as I transform back into a human.

Briskly, I walk down the hallway towards the nearest exit, aching for freedom from this living nightmare until sudden I stop dead in my tracks. There, staring down at me, are the new laboratory security cameras.

All of that work I spent avoiding exposure was for nothing, because I know for a fact that the second I get home, the Department of Homeland Security will come knocking within the hour. Everything has been caught on tape; my security breach, the nanobot exposure, and even my supernatural transformation into a sexy helicopter.

I let out a long sigh, defeated, until I'm suddenly hit with yet another idea.

The security office is close by, and the hard drives that record these video feeds are sitting out in the open, just waiting for me to unplug them and take off without a trace of evidence left behind. Theft of Buttcorp, and government, property only adds to the long list of problems I already have to deal with, but I've already gone too far to stop now. Besides, the second I step out that door I'm technically stealing myself.

Without a moment to spare, I turn on my heels and head back towards the security office.

When I arrive, I'm met with yet another hurtle. The office is not only locked, but currently being manned by a young velociraptor, fresh out of college and about my age. The dino stares blankly at his computer screen. I can only see him through a small slit of glass in the room's door, but from this angle I can plainly manage to make out the subtle reflection of hardcore gay porn reflecting off of the man's stylish eyewear.

"Shit." I say aloud, spotting the hard drives of security footage that sit on the shelf behind him, slowly filling with data.

Once again my brain flips into emergency mode, coolly assessing the options at hand, of which there are very few. If I was a bombshell like Donald, I could simply walk in there, give the new guy a few playful winks and then take the drive without him even batting an eye. However, these day's I'm having trouble even getting noticed at all, let alone ogled and lusted after.

Suddenly, it hits me. Maybe now, I *can* be a bombshell like Donald.

I focus intently on the internal workings of my body once again, only this time I start to let my imagination run wild. I picture my arms transforming into massive, steel blades, I imagine myself with perfectly toned curves that turn my body into a spherical metal and glass frame, and a set of abs that would make jaws drop.

Once again, my transformation is painless, but strange. It doesn't take long, and suddenly I find myself pulling out my phone to get a look at my imagination's handwork with the front-facing camera.

The results are shocking, to say the least, and absolutely surreal. There is a completely different being staring back at me from the tiny screen of my phone, an unrecognizable helicopter face that, had I seen out on the street, would more than likely fill me with bitterness than excitement at its pure, almost surreal mechanical beauty. Instead, a slow smile now creeps across my new visage.

Filled with a pristine confidence, I rap hard against the security office door with one of my blades.

It takes a while for the new guy to zip up his pants, but eventually he saunters over and throws open the door angrily. The second that he sees my face, however, everything changes.

"Whoa." The guy says, dumbstruck by my vehicular beauty.

His reaction is so severe that it takes me off guard for a moment. Is this really what it's like to be a handsome living object?

For the first few seconds I freeze up, the two of us standing here in awkward silence as we stare at each other. The man's change in demeanor is so severe that my initial reaction is to assume that he's joking, my brain barely able to accept the possibility that he could be that taken with my outward appearance.

"Hey there." I finally say. "What are you watchin'?"

The guy hesitates, still incredibly unsure of himself. "Nothing." He finally says. "Security footage. Can I help you?"

"Oh yeah?" I coo, ignoring his question and reaching down to take the name tag on his uniform between my cool copter blades. "Does Tucker know what you're doing in here while you're supposed to be paying attention, Greg?"

Greg plays dumb. "I don't know what you're talking about."

"You're not watching porn in here, are you?" I ask, giving him a little wink. "Because that's kinda what it looked like to me."

The raw sexual power that I wield now as a helicopter would be intoxicating enough, but in the hands of someone who's been celibate from billionaire dinosaurs for two years, like myself, it's like giving a baby the keys to a nuclear arsenal. I try to pull myself back a bit, to restrain my thoughts from disappearing too far down the rabbit hole of lust and excitement, but it's already too late. I don't care if he's rich or poor; any velociraptor is close enough.

"No, I wasn't watching porn." Greg scoffs, trying a little too hard to feign his innocence. "Who are you? I haven't seen you around the lab before."

I think for a moment, pursing my lips. Suddenly, a name just comes to me. "Mr. Chibs Pratt." I tell him. "Well Greg, it's too bad you're not watching any porn in here, I love porn."

Greg's dumb dinosaur eyes suddenly light up as I say this. I notice now that he's literally shaking as he stands before me, cowering in the presence of such a gorgeously constructed vehicle. "You do?" He stammers.

"Oh yeah." I say, pushing up against him as I make my way into the room and shutting the door behind me. "It makes me so fucking horny."

I'm lying. I haven't watched a porno in years thanks to my sex-addicted prehistoric celibacy, but from what I remember it all seemed a little too fake to me. I suppose there's a time and a place for that kind of thing, but it's not like I'm dying for it on a daily basis.

Greg however, is completely eating it up. I have him in the palm of my blade already, but teasing him like this is so much fun that I continue laying it on thick.

"Want to show me?" I ask in a deep, helicopter tone.

"Show you?" The security officer responds, his face turning bright red.

I laugh. "The porno you were watching. Maybe I could help you take a load off or something."

Suddenly, sobriety alarm bells are going off deep within my brain. I can't relapse, and as fun as this is I'm drifting dangerously close to the edge. It doesn't help matters that Greg the velociraptor is actually pretty cute in an unassuming kind of way.

I just need to get the drive and get out of here, I reaffirm, collecting my thoughts.

"Sure. I guess you can see it if you really want." Greg offers, walking back around the desk and sitting down in his chair. An image is paused on the laptop screen, and as I follow Greg and stand behind him I suddenly find myself with a perfect view. On there computer is the hardcore depiction of a T-Rex and a jet plane in the troughs of passion, there bodies intertwined as this muscular, handsome guy penetrates the plane deeply.

Greg presses the spacebar and the images instantly come to life, dancing across the laptop screen in vivid colors of silver and green. The office is filled with exaggerated moans of pleasure.

Trying my best to focus, I reach back behind me with one hand and unplug the currently running hard drive, then carefully slide it off of the counter and slip it inside my lab coat.

I breathe out a sigh of relief, happy to have the evidence of my exposure secured, but as I turn to leave the office something stops me.

My eyes are now transfixed onto computer screen, following the beautiful porn star bodies as the rock together in a million shifting pixels. Greg looks up at me to see my reaction, and when he notices that I'm not recoiling in horror he smiles.

"Pretty hot, huh?" Greg asks.

I nod, not saying a word. I can suddenly feel one of my empty blades, unburdened by the hard drive, slipping its way down from Greg's shoulder and along his chest. Lower and lower it goes, drifting dangerously closer to the waistband of his jeans.

Greg's breathing is heavy now, and I can see that his member has swelled to an enormous size within the fabric of his pants, just waiting from me to set it free. Greg repositions himself uncomfortably, aching to be touched.

"Need a hand?" I ask him.

"Yes." Greg sighs, and then begins to undo his belt buckle.

I realize now that I'm shaking with, not only anticipation, but fear. It's been years since I've seen a thick green dinosaur cock, and with good reason. My abstinence means too much to me to just throw it away, but seeing the lust in Greg's eyes is just so hard to turn down. I've never known what it was like to be seen like this; as a prize, a trophy, a helicopter.

Still, I need to stop.

I try and retract my hand, but my subconscious desires let it drift lower and lower across Greg's bare reptilian abs. He let's out a soft whimper as my fingers creep under the waistband of his boxer briefs.

Stop. I tell myself, but it's no use.

I feel my helicopter blade wrap slowly around his massive, rock hard rod and the two of us gasp at the same time. Greg sinks back into his chair and closes his eyes, letting out a long sigh of satisfaction as he reels from the sensation of my cool touch.

Suddenly, the gravity of what I'm doing hits me like a ton of bricks. I'm sick to my stomach as I release Greg from my grasp, immediately turning around and heading for the door of the office.

"Hey! Where are you going?" The young security officer shouts in startled confusion.

The next thing I know, I'm barreling down the hallway towards the back exit of the Buttcorp facility, tears streaming down my face despite my best efforts to keep them contained within.

I hit the exit door hard and suddenly a loud, blaring alarm is sounding in my ears. I immediately send my blades into a furious spin, propelling myself up into the sky. Almost immediately, I hear voices shouting below and I turn back around to see Tucker and some armed military personal standing at the doorway. Fortunately, the last place that they look is up and by the time they do I have long since disappeared in the great blue.

I fly across the city as fast as I can, finally landing in my own front yard and then immediately turning back into a human before anyone has a chance to notice.

4 CONFESSIONS OF A DINOSAUR GAMBLER

"My name is John Hams and I'm a billionaire dinosaur sex addict." I tell the group, sitting in my familiar spot in the church basement on Hollywood Blvd.

"Hi John Hams." The group responds in turn.

"It's been one day since my last sexual encounter." I announce.

The silence is deafening. I look around the circle of familiar faces and see that all of them are staring back at me in complete shock. For two years, I had been one of the most solid members here, the last person that anyone would expect to relapse. I guess it happens to everyone as some point.

Forbok and me lock eyes for a moment and, despite his best efforts to hide it, he looks utterly heartbroken; understanding, but heartbroken non-the-less.

"I relapsed last night." I continue. "Pretty hard, actually."

There is a long pause as I try to collect my thoughts. The events of the last few days are just too unbelievable, and potentially dangerous, to share. Even though these meetings are the safest environments that I know, I need to tread carefully.

"I found myself in situation that I'm not really used to." I explain. "This dinosaur really wanted me, and not just because he wanted to fuck someone. He really, really wanted *me*."

"We're you flattered by that?" Forbok asks.

"I was. I mean, it felt really nice to have someone reacting to me in a powerful way, even if he was just a regular dinosaur and not a billionaire." I

25

tell him. "But at the same time, in the back of my head I knew that it wasn't me he was attracted to."

Forbok shakes his head. "I'm not quite sure what you mean." He tells me, his expression one of someone who's desperately trying to relate. He really does care about me, I can see it in his eyes, and in this storm of confusion that crashes about in my head, it's nice to know that he's there trying to shine a light.

"He liked me, but I was pretending to be someone else." I tell him. "I'm not that guy anymore, but I slipped because it was just so easy to fall back into the old ways."

"The man that you were two years ago?" Forbok questions.

"Yes." I nod. "I'd forgotten what it felt like to let myself go like that, only this time was different. This time I had so much more power than before."

"Well, we need to accept that we're powerless against our impulses sometimes." Forbok tells me.

I've heard that a million times around here, and of all the pieces of advice that get thrown around, this is the only one that really kind of rubs me the wrong way. I'm a fighter, and I know that I've got the power to change my life. In fact, sometimes it's that faith in myself that keeps me going.

Or maybe I just don't truly understand this part of our mantra yet.

"I know." I lie to him, nodding. I don't even want to get into it tonight, there's way too much going on in my head to be focused on the semantics of our sexaholic code.

"You're always going to be you." Forbok says, looking me dead in the eyes.

It immediately strikes me how bizarrely relevant his comment is, but also how terrifyingly untrue. At this point, I can be whoever the fuck I want, a helicopter or a human.

"But what if…" I stammer, my words faltering. I'm getting emotional but I don't know why. After taking a minute to collect myself, I try again. "But what if I didn't have to be me anymore?" I ask. "Or what if I got to be me and the addict was someone else entirely?"

Forbok still doesn't follow what I'm saying, but he tries his best. "Either way, we'll support you right here in this room. We're all struggling, John Hams, but this is your family and we're gonna support you."

With that, the group bursts into a pleasant applause.

"Thank you." I tell them, and I mean it.

After our sharing session, I make my way over to the snack table yet again, still dreading my return to work the next day, but for entirely different reasons. Buttcorp has left three messages about speaking with me the second I get into the lab, and it wasn't until I called them back to confirm an eight AM conference that they left me alone.

I have no idea what they've found to connect me to the break-in back at the lab, but no matter how optimistic I try to be, this meeting can't be good.

"That was pretty powerful stuff tonight." Comes a familiar voice, as Yorb steps up next to me and pops a baby carrot into his stegosaurus mouth. His charm is so weirdly effortless, I can't even begin to understand it.

"Thanks." I tell the dinosaur. "It's weird starting back down here at the bottom again. Two years is a long time."

Yorb nods. "Well, it happens. The world keeps spinning."

The way he looks into me is incredible, and it suddenly hits me that Yorb is genuinely interested, heart and soul. It's not at all the way that the security officer had leered at my elegantly crafted helicopter body the night before, and the difference couldn't be more apparent.

Still, there's that mystery and silence to Yorb that I find so incredibly sexy. He's powerful, yet reserved; needing validation from no one.

It was a mistake to turn him down the other night. I'm trying to abstain from random, meaningless sex; but if I find the right partner this could all be over. I'd forgotten that, but after my relapse I've received a powerful reminder of the difference between these two distinct kinds of attraction. Not all dinosaurs are the same.

"Hey, so I was thinking…" I start, trying to summon all of the courage that I can.

Suddenly, Forbok joins us, saddling up next to Yorb and putting his arm around the prehistoric beast.

"That was really brave of you to share today." Forbok tells me. I try to look him in the eyes but I can't stop staring at his arm, which is draped around Yorb's shoulders and pulling the handsome dinosaur close.

"Thanks." I tell him, meekly.

Yorb turns to face Forbok and gives him a quick peck on the lips, then the two of them smile at each other before turning back towards me.

"I'm sorry, what were you saying?" Yorb asks.

I'm too stunned to speak, my jaw hanging slack as I try to comprehend the scene that's playing out right before my eyes. "I'm sorry." I ask. "Are you guys... dating?"

Forbok nods and then answers plainly. "We are."

I can't help the confused expression that creeps across my face. "Aren't we here because of our... sex addiction?"

Forbok laughs. "We're not having sex!" He informs me. "We're dating. There's a big difference."

I'm still in shock, but thankfully I manage to lock down my look of amazement before it shifts into one of utter disappointment. I've missed out on an incredible opportunity with a real genuine dinosaur. I know Forbok, and I know that he wouldn't put up with anything less.

"You know, John Hams, the reason for this group is to help people abstain from sex." Forbok continues. "Not abstain from real connection."

He's right.

"You still haven't asked me your question." Yorb adds, genuinely curious. "What's up?"

I feel like a deer in headlight as I stand before the two of them, rejected already before I even got the chance to ask Yorb out. My mind races with something else to say, trying to save myself the embarrassment that I'm helplessly barreling towards.

"I was going to ask..." I begin, still not exactly sure were my words are going to end up.

Yorb and Forbok wait patiently for me to finish. Suddenly, I'm hit with the perfect excuse.

"Oh!" I shout, startling them. "I was going to ask if you could give me a ride home tonight. I left my car at work yesterday and had to take the bus here."

Yorb smiles. "Oh yeah, of course. What part of town do you live in?"

"Peach Park." I tell him.

"Sure thing." Yorb confirms. "I'm downtown, so that's no problem at all."

"I'm gonna go say some more goodbyes." Forbok informs us, before giving Yorb another quick kiss. "I'll see you at dinner tomorrow." He tells him.

"The Hearth, seven thirty." Yorb responds with a smile.

The Hearth is one of the nicest new restaurants in Los Angeles, way beyond the price range of all but the most successful Hollywood elite. I would have never pegged Yorb as being all that wealthy thanks to his rugged, dinosaur look, complete tonight with well fitted jeans and a black leather jacket, but I guess I was mistaken.

"Are you ready to get out of here?" Yorb asks me.

I nod and we start heading for the door.

As Yorb and I step out into the warm night air, I can't help but be taken by his prehistoric stride, so controlled and yet so fierce. The church parking lot is still empty, with most of our fellow members still milling about and socializing inside.

Yorb presses his keys and a red sports car next to us beeps twice.

"Oh my god." I ask, unable to hide my shock. "Is this yours?"

Yorb nods and then tosses me the keys. "You want to drive it?"

I look down at the metallic ring and then back at Yorb. "Are you fucking serious? This is a half a million dollar car."

Yorb shrugs and then climbs inside the passenger seat, leaving me to stand in the parking lot speechless.

"I thought you wanted a ride home!" Yorb calls out from the inside of the car, laughing.

I open the door and carefully climb inside, suddenly painfully aware that I had been wrong about this dinosaur from the start, he is most definitely a billionaire.

"Welcome!" Says a woman's disembodied voice as I enter the vehicle. It starts automatically.

"What the fuck just happened?" I ask.

"The car knows that I'm here." Yorb laughs, seemingly just as amused as I am. It's the first time I've really seen him crack his calm and collected shell, but the moment is fleeting and almost immediately he's back to his usual thoughtful self.

"You know the way back to your place from here?" Yorb asks.

I nod.

"Then go for it!" He tells me. "Have fun."

I very carefully start to pull the car out of the church parking lot, going about half the speed that I normally would as I try my best not to damage anything on the terrifyingly expensive vehicle. Yorb eyes me from the passenger seat, trying desperately to keep a grin from creeping its way across his face.

"You know, sometimes driving too carefully can be even more dangerous." He tells me.

I stop the car. "Then why are you letting me drive this thing?" I ask him, exasperated.

Yorb smiles. "Why not? Taking risks is fun."

I shake my head, "I'm sorry, I'm too scared that I'm going to fuck this car up."

Suddenly, a car is honking from behind us, pulling me back into reality as I realize that I've stopped right in the middle of the street.

Yorb gets out and waves them past, then comes over to my side and opens the door for me. "Maybe next time." He says cheerfully.

As we cruise down the Hollywood freeway my eyes are transfixed on Yorb, who stares intently forward through the windshield as the city lights dance across his face. In Yorb's claw is a large silver coin, which he rolls between his fingers effortlessly, as if he's been doing it for years.

"What's with the coin?" I ask him. "I always see you flipping it during our meetings."

Yorb grins, but doesn't take his eyes off the road. "It's just a reminder."

"A reminder of what?" I pry.

"That there are two sides to everything." He tells me, and then finally glances over. "Everyone."

"Tell me about it." I laugh, leaning back into my seat and shutting my eyes. I'm exhausted, stressed, and as fun as it is being in the presence of such a satisfyingly handsome and mysterious dinosaur, I still have work to look forward too tomorrow. For all I know, this could be the last day of my life outside of government quarantine.

I let out a long sigh.

"What up?" Yorb asks.

"Work stuff." I tell him, simplifying things to comical absurdity.

"Ah," he says in understanding. "I hear you."

I can't help but flash Yorb a slight smirk. "How old are you?" I ask him.

"I'm guessing the same age as you." He tells me. "Twenty-five."

"Twenty-four." I respond. "So how the fuck is it that a twenty-five year old comes to be driving a car like this? I'm sorry, but I get the feeling it's not due to any work of your own. Where are your parents?"

Yorb stops spinning his coin around his finger and pushes it into a crack in his dashboard, where it stays perfectly. "Dead." He tells me.

"Oh my god." I stammer. "I'm so sorry."

"No, it's fine." Yorb responds, "I mean, it's been over a decade now. They weren't wealthy though, if that's what you're thinking. All of this I earned on my own."

I'm shocked. "Really? That's incredible."

Yorb cracks a sharp-toothed smile. "Although, you're right about one thing, it wasn't really work."

"What do you mean?" I ask.

Yorb sighs. "I'm a gambler." He stops and corrects himself. "*Was* a gambler, I should say. Blackjack, slots, but mostly blackjack, that's where I made all of my money."

"Damn." I say. "Well, what happened?"

He laughs. "You're nosy!"

I recoil a bit.

"I'm sorry." Yorb tells me. "I mean, I'm gonna have to talk about all of this at a meeting one of these days anyway, might as well do it now. I had to give up the gambling when things started getting out of control."

I nod, completely understanding.

"The sex, the drugs, the whole lifestyle really. I was living in Vegas and playing in the high roller cash games, more money than I knew what to do with, but I wasn't happy." Yorb takes out the coin and starts flipping it through his fingers again, some kind of coping mechanism. "A was dating a jet plane card counter by the name of Keith. He was a good man, but he ended up leaving me for one of his passengers and it kind of sent me into a tailspin."

I watch Yorb's eyes as the memories seem to flood back to him.

"After me and Keith broke up I was out of control; started playing poker on the side in some games that I shouldn't have been in. One night I took a guy for about five million dollars in one game of poker, which he didn't really seem to care about all that much. When I took his boyfriend later, though, that's when things got ugly."

Yorb lifts up his shirt to reveal three large scars in his side, as well as a

31

glimpse at his utterly impeccable abs. He's toned beyond belief under there.

"He was a T-Rex. Huge bites right here, head smashed, broken legs." Yorb tells me. "I should be dead but an old woman found me lying out behind the Casino when she used the wrong exit door, thinking it was the way to the cashier. She was trying to cash in a token that she'd found on the floor."

Yorb hands me the token. On one side there is a chiseled man's face, and on the other is the image of dollar sign with some words etched below it.

I carefully read the inscription out loud. "The Keen Dangler Casino, One Dollar. She was trying to cash a one dollar token?" I ask.

Yorb laughs. "Actually, she thought it was for a hundred. Really bad eyesight on the poor woman, but lucky for me."

"Whoa." I say. "You seem so calm and collected, I can't even imagine you being out of control of yourself."

"Well, you're kinda right." Yorb sighs. "I mean, that's why I was so good at gambling. I can keep my feelings locked up pretty well, but when you do that they have a tendency to get sneaky and turn into bad habits. That's what the coins for, to remind me that there are two sides to everyone, even myself."

I nod. "You're right."

Yorb glances over at me again, something flickering behind his stegosaurs eyes. "This is crazy, I've never talked about this stuff with anyone before."

I blush slightly. "Glad I could help to open up the floodgates."

The two of us are silent for a moment. I can tell that Yorb is thinking long and hard about something important, weighing the pros and cons in his head. "Hey, are you hungry?" He finally asks.

I smile. "Sure, let's grab something."

5 SWALLOWED WHOLE

The din of the restaurant feels good within my ears, a pleasant hum to momentarily block out all of the anxiety I've been swimming in over the last few days. The place is inviting, a classic kind of late night diner where the waitresses never forget to come back and refill your coffee.

Yorb sits across from me in his usual confident relaxed state, leaning back against the booth with one scaly arm draped lazily behind him. He has the incredible ability to fit in anywhere, from a cheap burger joint to a five star restaurant. I can't imagine the dinosaur being anything but comfortable in his own thick hide, the exact thing that I'm not these days.

There lies an intensity behind his eyes, however, that's unmistakable. Yorb is interested in me, and not just as a sexual being (although, that's certainly in there as well). He's curious; excited.

"Remember the first meeting?" Yorb asks. "When I asked you about your job?"

"Yeah, I do." I tell him, taking a sip from my coffee. I crack a smile. "Why? You want to know about my job now?"

Yorb laughs. "No. I just want to know about you."

I can feel a slight tugging within my heart, a tiny chill that runs down my spine. "What do you want to know?"

Yorb is silent for a moment, his yellow eyes narrowing a bit as he sizes me up. He's trying to determine my tolerance for his prodding, but it doesn't take him long to make up his mind and dive in; a true risk taker.

"Tell me about why you've been going to meetings for two years." He says.

I look down instinctively; my identity exposed and dragged up onto the chopping block. You'd think after all of this time, all of this sharing, I would finally be about to express myself about what brought me to this sad, lonely place in my life.

"I was married once." I tell Yorb.

He seems slightly confused, but does his best not to show it.

"I know," I laugh. "We we're only eighteen years old, high school sweethearts, actually."

"Sounds kinda nice." Yorb says. "Settling down that early and not having to worry about all of this bullshit."

I nod. "I was, at first. But the thing about getting married to someone that early in life is that you really don't know them, and people can change a lot. Even the sweetest dinosaurs can get dark and bitter, especially when they come from a family of alcoholics."

"Don't I know it." Yorb tells me. "My father was the perfect Jurassic gentleman until he had a couple of beers in him."

"There's two sides to everyone." I say, throwing his own line back at him.

Yorb continues listening, but instinctively pulls out his coin as I speak, and then starts flipping it across his claws quietly.

"Anyway, as we got older, my husband, Waldo, started to change. In our youth his petty T-Rex jealousy just came off as childish, something that would eventually blow over as he matured and started to figure himself out, but it only got worse as time went on and the liquor kept flowing. His family was incredibly wealthy and they enabled him. Where any other dinosaur would have hit rock bottom long ago, Waldo's mother and father kept bailing him out. Thanks to them, my husband never learned from any of his mistakes."

Yorb is listening intently, hanging on every word that comes out of my mouth. There's something incredibly charming about his attention, and I suddenly can't remember the last time a creature truly listened to me like this.

"It wouldn't have been so bad if he wasn't cheating on me, as well." I continue, my hands literally starting to shake as I recall the way that I was treated by my ex. "I mean, the fucking nerve."

Yorb reaches across the table and puts his claw over my hand, which instantly calms me like a beautiful wave of medicine for my soul. The shaking stops and I immediately return to reality.

"It's okay." Yorb tells me. "You don't need to get into it like that. I understand."

"No." I tell him. "It's good to get it out."

Yorb nods.

"One day when Waldo was out seeing one of his regular hook ups, I left the house and went to the store. I ran into an old friend from high school who I hadn't seen in years. He was always such a nice guy back then." I stop for a moment and stare off out the diner window. "I was so sad and lonely, so I brought him home and we started to fool around. It's the first time that I had felt desirable in months; the first time I felt like a real man, even."

Yorb closes his eyes, as if he already knows what's about to come next.

"The next thing I know." I continue. "Waldo is smashing through the door and he's pissed off; I mean really fucking pissed off."

I start shaking again, and this time Yorb's hand can't do anything to calm me. I keep going though, willing myself to push through the trauma and come out safely on the other side.

"I remember screaming." I say, a single tear rolling down my cheek. "And then I remember Waldo opening his jaws and eating my friend, just swallowing him whole in one massive T-Rex bite."

"Oh my god." The words fall out of Yorb's mouth and land on the table before him. He's in utter shock, his heart aching for me as he sits across the table and listens so intently; so carefully.

"That's when Waldo turned to me and opened wide." I say. "I remember looking him in the eye and thinking, what happened to this man that I loved? The guy who would do anything for me? How did he become this entirely new person?" I laugh to myself. "But I guess there are two sides to every coin."

We sit in silence for a moment, the air electrified by the emotion that buzzes between us.

"So what happened?" Yorb finally asks.

I snap out of it suddenly, as if the thought had never ever even occurred to me. "Oh." I start. "The neighbors showed up, shot him with a few tranquilizer darts."

"That fast?" Yorb repeats back to me in utter shock.

"Lady luck, I guess." I tell him. "I haven't had sex since that day.

Even the thought of it makes me sick. I'm still attracted to billionaire dinosaurs, but they scare me. No offence."

"None taken." Yorb says. The dinosaur is dumbfounded, but his expression alone makes me feel warm and safe. Obviously, I've made mistakes before when it comes to prehistoric beasts, but this guy is different.

Suddenly, though, Yorb's expression starts to change, he's looking down at my arm and wearing a face that goes from concern to downright confusion.

I immediately glance down to see what he's looking at. My emotional explosion must have caused a slight corruption in the nanobot code, because my body is stretching and morphing again, just like back in the lab. The flesh of my left arm seems to be stretching out away from my body on its own accord, extending in a strange line that creeps along through the air like a metallic helicopter blade.

"Fuck!" I shout, jumping up from the booth and knocking over my coffee, which spills across the table with a loud clatter.

Everyone in the restaurant turns to look at us as I cover my arm with the opposite hand and rush straight for the restroom.

"John Hams! Are you okay?" Yorb shouts from behind me, first trying to follow and then turning back to contain the coffee spill with several napkins.

"Yeah, I'm fine! I just need a minute, I'll be right back." I tell him frantically.

I burst through the restroom door and head straight for the mirror. I can already see parts of my face stretching out into windshield glass as the nanobot glitch continues to blossom within me, literally tearing me apart. Could this be the end?

I grab the edge of the sink to support myself, staring back at my rapidly distorting reflection in the mirror and trying desperately to calm down. My breathing heavy and my heart slamming within my chest, I find my body in a losing battle against the corruption of my new biomechanical cells.

Closing my eyes, I focus on collecting myself, finding a center internally that I can grab onto for just one fleeting moment. There is a calm within the center of this tornado, and when I find it I latch on tight. I remind myself that the only way through this is by staying grounded, and then I open my eyes.

The strange helicopter-like mutations are now retracting back into my body, returning to the steady form of their initial programming. I let out a sigh of relief, running my hand across my skin as it fully returns to normal.

Suddenly, Yorb is pushing through the door of the restroom behind me. Without a word he grabs me in his large, muscular arms and holds me tight, our bodies pressed together in a show of love and support that immediately fills me with warmth. I'm crying again, but not the same wild tears of frenzied emotion from before; I'm crying out of appreciation, and loss. This is one of the most incredible dinosaurs I have ever met; understanding, supportive, and most of all, honest. I was such an idiot to turn him away when I did, but I had forgotten that when I closed myself off gay sexually, I also closed off my heart.

Unfortunately, I've realized this when I might only have days left to live, the nanobots threatening to give way at any moment and rip me apart like nothing more than a string of faulty computer code.

I sink deeper into Yorb's supportive embrace, taking in his masculine presence.

"Are you alright?" Yorb finally whispers. "I'm sorry, we don't have to talk about the past anymore."

"I'm fine." I tell him. "It wasn't you. I just have this... skin thing."

Yorb doesn't say anything in return, but he seems to buy it; for now at least.

Finally, I pull away from this breathtakingly handsome man and look up into his eyes. We connect instantly, an excitement flowing between us that simply can't be denied. I lift up onto my tiptoes and slowly push my lips towards his.

"I'm sorry." Yorb says, pulling again.

Disappointment hits me like a ton of bricks. "What is it?" I ask.

Yorb stares back at me with an achingly sad, but stern, look in his eyes. "I can't." He says. "I'm dating Forbok. I'm not the kind of guy who does this anymore."

I want to fight for this, to try and talk Yorb out of it somehow, but I already know that it's no use. Yorb's mind is a strong one, well trained after long hours of controlled emotion at the poker table.

"I understand." I tell him, lying through my teeth, and then go in for another long, supportive hug.

I never want to leave this position, but eventually the muscular stegosaurus pulls away and leads me back to our booth, where he pays and then the two of us leave in silence.

The rest of the drive back to my place is quiet, both Yorb and me lost in our own mess of deep, swirling thoughts.

As much as this billionaire beast says he's attracted to me, and as much as I believe him when he looks deep into my eyes, I can't help but think that if I truly mattered to him he would break things off with Forbok right then and there. Of course, this is just me being selfish and I know it, but I can't help myself.

I also can't help thinking that if Forbok wasn't standing in the way, I could be starting the first day of the rest of my life tonight, taking the easy road to recovery with a fellow addict and, when the time was right, finally having a sexual relationship with someone that wasn't built on darkness and self loathing.

What the fuck did Forbok have that I didn't, anyway?

I just can't help it any longer. The big green monster of jealousy has consumed me and I'm completely at its whim, overwhelmed by the desire to have Yorb entirely for myself. If only him and Forbok could just realize that they weren't really compatible and get this whole charade over with.

I suppose, however, that there are ways I could speed up the process.

The second that I think this awful thought I immediately try to push it away and lock the gates behind it. I've spent the last two years making every decision as thoughtfully and morally as I can, and I'm not about to let that change over some dinosaur that, real talk, I only just met. Still the feeling lingers within me, and the longer that Yorb and I ride in silence, the more powerful it grows.

The dam within my soul is leaking, I suddenly realize, cracked open when I relapsed the other day in the security office. The gay sexual machine that has been lurking within me is anxious to get out, ready to explode forth and devour everything in its path after all of these years pent up and alone.

Who am I to stand in its way?

"Arrived." Says a feminine, disembodied voice over Yorb's stereo system.

We've pulled up outside of my modest, Echo Park apartment, a place in the driveway still empty as my car remains marooned at the Buttcorp parking long.

"Thanks for coffee." I tell Yorb with a smile.

He laughs and grins back. "No problem, maybe next time we can actually stick around long enough for dinner."

I try to keep up my cheerful charade but I can't, immediately realizing that there won't be a next time. Yorb is with Forbok now.

I start to climb out of his car and then stop myself, turning back around.

"Hey, do you have a sponsor yet?" I ask.

"Yeah." Yorb nods. "Bruce, the older guy with the tattoos."

"Okay, good." I confirm. "Well, thanks again for tonight, it was really nice talking to you."

Yorb gives me a playful wink that sends a sharp chill of desire down my spine. "Don't mention it." He tells me.

I close the door and watch as his gorgeous red sports car disappears completely around the next street corner, then immediately walk as briskly as possible to a payphone at the nearby connivance store.

I immediately dial Bruce's phone number.

As the phone's receiver begins to ring back at me through the headset, I focus on putting on the best fake Yorb voice that I possibly can.

"Hello?" I practice aloud, my tone dropping a full octave to get that dinosaur cadence. I try again, tightening things up as I go. "Hello? Hello?" I play with the word in my mouth, trying to find my best approximation of Yorb's voice until Bruce answers abruptly.

"This is Bruce." Comes the man's voice on the other end of the line.

"Hey there, it's Yorb." I say, impressed by the tone that I've been able to craft for myself.

"Yorb?" Bruce asks, noticing something strange in my voice. "Is everything alright?"

"No man." I tell him. "I need you to come over here."

"Shit." Bruce says, fully alert now. "I'm on my way."

"Wait!" I tell him. "I'm in my second loft downtown, you have the address to this one?"

"You've got more than one place down there? Let me see here." Bruce says, pulling his phone away form his mouth for a moment. I can hear some papers rustling around in the background. "Okay, the address I have is 472 Main St. Apartment #1507, is that the one?"

A devilish smile crosses my face. "Yeah, that's it." I say, my voice cracking slightly.

"Yorb?" Bruce asks, a sudden stab of skepticism in his throat. "This is Yorb isn't it?"

"I... Um." I stammer, losing my concentration.

"Who the fuck is this?" Bruce demands to know.

"I'm sorry, I think I'm actually gonna be fine tonight." I tell Bruce. "Don't worry about coming by."

I hang up the phone and then step back, giving myself enough room to center myself and then quickly transform into a handsome helicopter.

I take off immediately into the air of this warm, Los Angeles night, heading straight for downtown. I'm terrified by my actions, yet somehow impressed by my own devious resourcefulness.

6 CAUGHT IN THE COCKPIT

I reach the door of Yorb's building and push through into the luxurious lobby.

There's usually a doorman, but it's too late for that right now. Instead, a security guard waits for me at a large oak desk. He nods and waves me on. I've already entered the gate code, and this man's job is much more about keeping out transients than play detective. Besides, how's he supposed to keep track of every resident in this massive downtown skyscraper?

Unlike most of the buildings down here, this place is brand new; beautiful, shiny and modern. As I cross the lobby, I can't help but admire all of the upscale furnishings.

I reach the elevator and then step inside, pressing the button marked fifteen, which is where Yorb's penthouse is located. When the door slides closed in front of me I nearly jump out of my skin as I lock eyes the helicopter staring back.

I am no longer John Hams; that entire shell stripped away and replaced by that of the most ravishing aircraft I could ever hope to dream up, Chibs Pratt. I give myself a little wink in the elevator door's reflection, still impressed by my incredible new machinery.

Wondering if Yorb prefers a chopper in dark gunmetal or light tan, I adjust the color of my paint job accordingly and then settle back on my original, seductive matte black look. I also suddenly remember that this building, like the one at the lab, probably has security cameras and I'd be wise not to make any more sudden changes to my appearance.

The door lets out a pleasant ping as it opens up onto the fifteen floor, which has only a small hallway due to the enormous size of the lofts. I step out on my landing skids and walk down the ornate carpet a little ways until I reach unit 1507, then knock loudly with a blade.

After a moment I hear the shuffle of footsteps from somewhere deep within, then abruptly the door is unlocked and swinging inward.

"Can I help you?" Yorb asks. The startled man stops abruptly when he sees me. He tries his best not to glance down at my incredibly ripped helicopter abs, but Yorb is only dino. His gaze doesn't linger however, and moments later he's collected himself enough to hold a conversation.

"Hi." I say, smiling. "I'm Chibs. Your neighbor upstairs."

Yorb looks confused. "Are you new? I've never seen you."

I nod. "Just moved in. I love the building, I'm so happy to be here but there's just one problem."

I let my comment linger in the air for a moment until Yorb finally takes the bait and asks. "What is it?"

"Well, I'm trying to sleep right now, and all the noise down here is keeping me awake." I say.

"Noise?" Now Yorb is really confused. "What noise?"

I roll my helicopter eyes playfully. You don't have to be embarrassed, the whole building can hear you fucking in there."

Yorb can't help but burst out laughing as I say this. "I'm sorry, but you definitely have the wrong guy. There's no fucking going on in here."

"Well, you don't have to admit it, but I can hear it through the vents and it's very loud. I need to get up early for work so if you could please keep it down, I'd appreciate it." I explain.

Yorb shakes his head. "I swear to you, there's no sex happening in here. I don't know which apartment the sound is coming from but it's not mine."

I take a step closer to Yorb now, crossing into his personal space and letting the electrify flow freely between us. "Listen, you're very handsome, so I'm sure you can invite him over again tomorrow when it's the weekend and the rest of us don't have to get up at the crack of dawn. I'm not trying to ruin the fun, but please keep it down. I've got a lot of flights tomorrow."

Yorb is playfully frustrated now, not by the way this mysterious helicopter has just barged into his life unannounced, but by the simple fact that I refuse to believe him.

Finally, Yorb throws open his door all the way and steps to the side with a laugh. "I swear to you." He says. "Come see for yourself."

I shrug and cross over the threshold of Yorb's incredible luxury apartment, trying not to celebrate my small victory towards his inevitable seduction. I feel powerful in this perfect vehicular body that I've created, like anything is possible.

Yorb's place is phenomenally large; a well kept bachelor pad that's way bigger than it needs to be for just one man. The first room that we step into is a massive living room that overlooks the city below, the night skyline twinkling with a smattering of distant apartment lights from other people burning the midnight oil like ourselves. The ceiling is high, and I immediately realize that the place has two stories, which gives my story slightly less credibility.

"Look!" Yorb says, motioning over to the right. "My bedrooms not even upstairs, you couldn't have heard me anyway."

I pretend to be too preoccupied with the majestic city landscape to follow him, instead stepping forward until I'm right up against the massive, living room windows. I can see the slight reflection of my strange new self staring back at me, and watch as Yorb steps up behind.

"Your view is incredible." I tell him, my eyes remaining transfixed on the urban beauty that stretches out before me. "Reminds me of being in flight."

I catch Yorb making a confused face in the reflection. "Don't you have the same view from your apartment upstairs?" He asks.

"Yeah, I do." I respond, stumbling over my words a bit as I try to think fast. "I just mean… in general. It's an incredible city."

Yorb nods.

Not wanting to waste any more time, I turn around to face the handsome, rugged man and then slowly but surely begin to open my helicopter doors for him.

"Whoa! Hey!" Yorb says, reaching out to stop me. "What are you doing?"

He's holding my doors closed now, keeping me from revealing myself entirely, but instead of pushing me away the two of us just stand here, locked together.

I can feel Yorb's dinosaur heart thumping in his chest, clearly trying is best to keep it together around such an incredibly attractive vehicle.

"You should go." Yorb finally whispers. "I don't even know you, and this isn't me anymore. I've been with a living object before, but it's just too soon to try again."

"This isn't me either." I say, revealing more about the situation than he could ever truly understand.

Standing here in his embrace reminds me of the way that Yorb held me earlier at the diner, but this time there is something sinister blooming between us, something darker. I find myself wishing that he was seeing me for who I really was, not just this sexed up helicopter that I've created.

But that's not the real world, and the sooner I let go of that the better. At the end of the day Yorb is just a stegosaurus, I tell myself, and I need to accept that he'll never like me for who I really am. At least not with Forbok in the picture, anyway.

As Chibs Pratt, however, I have the chance to actually take a stand and do something about it.

I reach down and run my hand across Yorb's muscular green chest, moving slowly so as to appreciate every subtle curve of the man's toned body. He doesn't resist and, instead, closes his eyes as he reels from the long lost sensation of a vehicle's touch. It's easy to forget that Yorb's resisted this temptation for years now, which could be an obstacle for most men trying to seduce him, but with my perfect new body it only makes my sexuality even more powerful.

Should I feel bad for trying to get Yorb to relapse a start fucking aircraft again? Yes, I should. But I'm relapsing as well, albeit behind the safety of a manufactured character. These may be my cells and their nanobot counterparts, but they're not arranged in any way that truly resembles what is it to be John Hams. I'm disconnected now, free from responsibility and guilt; free to fuck and fight and live any way that I please.

"I want you." I say, letting my hand drift lower and lower until it reaches Yorb's belt buckle, which I unclasp.

"I want you, too." He says, finally giving in.

I undo his belt, then slowly unzip Yorb's pants which I can see now were hastily thrown on when I woke him up, because there's no underwear beneath.

Instead, I'm greeted by this sight of his throbbing green member, which springs forth from the fabric as soon as I let it. Yorb's hard as a rock and aching to be touched, his enormous stegosaurus cock jutting fiercely out towards me.

I smile and slowly drop down into a squat before Yorb, so that his shaft is pointed directly at my gorgeous face, and then look up at him with my big soulful eyes.

"Do you want me to suck you off?" I ask playfully, once again feeling confident and sultry in my new body.

Yorb doesn't answer, clearly struggling with some internal demons.

"I said, do you want me to suck off that big, fat cock of yours?" I repeat.

Finally, Yorb breaks his silence; the single word barely making it out of his gently parted lips alive. "Yes."

With that, I open my helicopter mouth wide and engulf Yorb's cock with my mouth, pushing my head down along the length of his shaft until I reach the edge of my gag reflex. I close my eyes and focus, commanding the nanobots to change within my body ever so slightly until finally I feel comfortable going even deeper. Eventually, I reach the base of his shaft with my lips, my face pushed right up against Yorb's hard abs as he fills my throat entirely.

The man lets out a long, satisfied moan, his entire body shaking from my masterful deep throat. I can feel Yorb's hands press gently on the back of my head and hold me there, hesitating, as if he's still not entirely sure that he wants to commit to this.

But the ship has already sailed, and as I reach up and begin to play with his hanging dinosaur balls that rest against my chin, the feeling is just too much for Yorb to ignore. He starts to pump me up and down his shaft, slowly at first and then gaining speed as the waves of pleasure start to overwhelm him.

I look up at Yorb and we lock eyes, his cock planted firmly in my throat. I can't help but give him a playful little wink, and suddenly he's over the edge completely, a crazed look of sexual passion overwhelming his expression as he rocks his hips against me.

I slowly pull his pants father and farther down until he's able to step out of them, which is all that I need. Releasing Yorb from my mouth I stand up and give him a deep kiss.

"Go to the bedroom and lie down." I instruct.

Yorb starts to protest slightly but I'm firm with my instructions. I grab his claw with a blade and then force it down the front of my hull, letting him carass my incredible helicopter abs.

"If you want this body." I state plainly. "Then you can go into the bedroom and lie down."

With that, I step back from Yorb and watch as he heads for what I assume is his master bedroom, stripping off his shirt as he goes. Studying Yorb's muscular prehistoric frame sends a chill down my spine, his form a perfect specimen from head to tail.

I don't have much time to meditate on it, however, because the second he disappears into the other room I spring into action, dropping down and grabbing his crumpled pants off of the floor with a blade that I have now transformed into a human hand. I find his phone in the front pocket and pull it out immediately, relieved that there is no password lock, and then scroll through the contacts until I find Forbok's number.

'Need help. Come over now. Let yourself in.' I type, then hit send. The second that the message comes back to me as delivered I delete the entire text history and then turn off the phone, placing it back into Yorb's pocket.

Moments later, I enter the bedroom and find Yorb sprawled out on his bed before me, his cock hard and standing at full attention. It's much longer and thicker than I had even realized when it was engulfed within my mouth, and now that I can fully inspect the shaft's incredible size I'm even more impressed.

The room itself is massive, as well, with another set of windows that fill the far wall from floor to ceiling and look out towards the distant Hollywood Hills. It's a corner unit, providing two completely unique, but equally breathtaking, views.

I slowly strut across the hardwood floors on my landing skids towards Yorb, enjoying the way that his yellow dinosaur eyes flicker and dance across my metallic body. At this point, he can't help but stare.

Seductively, I give my blades a quick flash of speed and hover up onto the bed, then crawl towards him, eventually positioning myself directly over his body. I take Yorb's hands carefully with two blades and pull them above his head, controlling him completely as I make my way down his ripped chest and scaly abs with a series of sensual kisses.

Despite my newfound confidence, however, I find myself trembling with anticipation and fear. Through my new body I've been able to disconnect myself from my own actions, create a safe distance with the simple excuse that it's not actually me doing all of these erotic things. But Chibs Pratt and John Hams still share a brain, a soul; and the weight of that is still heavy upon me.

I close my eyes and take a deep breath, then let go of any reservations I had left within me. Immediately, I reach down and take Yorb's huge rod into my hand, aligning him with the tightness of my helicopter fuel pipe.

"Oh fuck." Yorb groans instinctively as I push down onto him, letting out a soft moan of my own as the powerful stegosaurus slides up inside of me.

His presence fills me with a sensation that is familiar and warm, a distant memory that had been locked away until this very moment. I bite my lip instinctively and start to grind against him with firm, deep swoops of my cockpit.

I'm not fully prepared for the long forgotten sensation of being entered by a man, and almost immediately I'm beside myself with pleasure, my body trembling and quaking as I ride him. It's as if all the sexual bliss that I've been staving myself from has been here the whole time, hiding away in some dark corner of my being and just waiting to be released by the right billionaire dinosaur.

"Oh my god." I pant loudly, repeating the words over and over again. "Oh my god, oh my god."

Yorb's hands are on my landing skids, helping to pull me up and down across him in an incredible pulsing rhythm. I can feel all of his powerful strength though this minor touch; he's showing restraint, his body handling me firmly but with care.

"Let go." I tell him. "Just fuck me like the prehistoric beast that you are."

Yorb looks up at me with a look of ferocious lust on his face, but also one of caution. Even now, as we sink deeper and deeper into our mutual relapses, he's trying to hold something close.

There's no turning back now, however, and Yorb is on the verge of confronting this reality for himself.

"Fuck my fuel pipe asshole!." I command, trying my best to give him that last little push. "Let go and give it to me like I know you want to."

Yorb closes his yellow eyes tight, one last attempt to shield himself against the powerful onslaught of sexual endorphins that flow through his veins, but when he opens his eyes again I can see that he's a changed man.

Suddenly, Yorb is sitting up and flipping me around with his muscular arms, turning me so that I'm facing away from him with my tail boom back over his shoulder. I look back at my dinosaur lover and smile.

There's a loud crack as Yorb slaps my ass, hard, then he grabs me by my tail rotor and pulls me back towards him with ease. He grabs his cock and maneuvers it into the entrance of my aching tightness. There's a fire in Yorb's eyes as he thrusts into me, the massive rod filling me entirely as I cry out with a yelp of pleasure. Yorb wastes no time now, immediately getting to work as he rams me from behind.

I grip tightly with my blades onto the bed sheets in front of me, bracing myself against Yorb's powerful slams. There is an animalistic nature to his thrusting now, more brazen than sensual, but the dinosaur still knows exactly where to hit me from the inside. Somehow, this is even more of a turn on than before, his gentlemanly demeanor finally cracking before my very eyes, the poker face slipping away and finally revealing the sexual beast underneath.

"Harder!" I scream back at him, never more turned on my entire life. "Fuck my helicopter asshole harder!"

Yorb doesn't need to be told twice, picking up speed until he is absolutely pummeling me with everything that he's got, slamming my butt from behind with completely reckless abandon.

Deep within my stomach I can now feel the first beautiful sparks of prostate orgasm begin to fly, lighting a tiny fire that slowly but surely begins to creep its way out across my body. I can't help but start to tremble and quake as the sensation consumes me, filling me with a strange warmth from head to toe.

I reach down with one blade between my skids and find my, hanging, rock hard cock. I grab it and begin to stroke ferociously, beating myself off in time with Yorb's powerful pumps.

The tremors of pleasant sensation keep coming in awesome waves, the space between them drawing shorter until finally it just becomes one giant ball of pleasure that envelopes my body. I clench my teeth tightly and let out a long hiss, frantically grasping at the last straws of reality before a powerful orgasm pushes me over the edge.

I'm outside myself now, looking down at my body cum ejects hard from the head of my massive helicopter cock. It's a satisfaction that can barely be described, a blinding fullness that consumes me perfectly. I throw my head back and let out a howl of ecstasy, unable to contain all of this sensation within.

Never before have a cum so hard that I achieved an out of body experience, and the sensation is exciting and new. However, as I look down at my own body in the troughs of orgasm, there is something strangely unsatisfying, a nagging disappointment at the fact that this vehicle below is not actually me, but a rearrangement of my cells to create something else; some unrealistically gorgeous aircraft.

I don't have long to mull on this, however, because seconds later Yorb is shaking as well, his body preparing for an orgasm of his own.

"Cum all over me!" I demand fiercely, doing my best porn star impression. "Shoot that load all over my cockpit!"

I open my doors and watch as Yorb immediately climbs inside, positioning himself before the control panel of flashing lights in the cockpit.

"Do it!" I scream. "Shoot your load all over the inside of this hot helicopter!"

Yorb gives his cock three final pumps with his hand, then grips tightly against the base as a rope of hot jizz ejects out across my flashing control panels. It feels nice against my metallic skin; playful almost, in it's erotic absurdly. To go from billionaire dinosaur abstinence to this in such a short time is almost too much for me to handle and I find myself chuckling with satisfaction.

Yorb throws his head back and closes his eyes tight, his abs held firm as several more pumps of cum eject from his shaft and splatter across me.

Suddenly, the door to the bedroom flies open, causing Yorb to turn immediately, frozen still with his dick gripped tightly as he stands in my cockpit.

"What the fuck is this?" Comes a familiar voice as Forbok steps out from the shadows, a look of sheer rage plastered across his face.

"Forbok!" Yorb says, his voice a mixture of more emotions than I can count.

"What are you doing?" Forbok asks, a slight hint of sadness shining through the anger as his voice wobbles slightly, losing its footing for a split second before falling back into line.

Yorb is not the type of dinosaur to run from his problems, and almost immediately I see him accept his fate. "I'm sorry." Is all that he says, a look of genuine remorse on his face. "I thought I'd changed, but I guess this is just who I am. I fuck living objects."

As I hear this my heart breaks, suddenly hit with the undeniable consequences of my actions. Sure Yorb and Forbok would certainly no longer be an item, but at what cost? Was it worth destroying our mutual sobriety like this for a moment of passion, especially given that the underlying motive was so dark?

Parked here on the bed, my panels covered in Yorb's dinosaur spunk, I suddenly realize that the persona of Chibs Pratt is already growing beyond my control.

"Who's the chopper?" Forbok asks Yorb.

He looks over at me, and then shakes his head. "I can't even remember his name."

"I'm Chibs Pratt." I offer. "I live upstairs."

Forbok just chuckles in utter disappointment. Yorb opens his mouth to say something but Forbok holds up his hand and stops him immediately. "Don't." He says. "I don't ever want to see you again. Please find a new meeting to attend, as well."

Yorb nods in understanding. "I'm sorry." He repeats.

Forbok just lets out a long sigh and shakes his head, then turns and walks back out the door, leaving Yorb in me to sit in silence.

"I think you should go." Yorb finally says.

7 THE VIDEO

One of the great advantages to shape shifting that I'd never considered previously, is that you never have to look hung-over or tired.

As I approach the Buttcorp building I'm many times more exhausted than I should be, given the importance that today could possibly have on the rest of my life, but from the outside you'd never know it. Baggy eyes; tightened up. Messy, slept on hair; fixed. Having nanobots attached to your cells is a dangerous game, one with many unknown consequence, but it's also pretty cool having a permanent method of perking yourself up.

I reach the front door and scan my card, which still doesn't work. With all of the craziness that occurred the last time I was here, I had completely forgotten to actually get my credentials updated.

I knock loudly and then wait for Tucker to arrive and push the door open.

"Can I help you?" He asks.

I immediately push past him. "I don't have time for you to remember who I am." I tell the man, impressing even myself with my newfound confidence.

"Wait a minute, sir!" The security guard shouts, following close behind me. "Stop right there."

I refuse to listen, instead heading straight for the conference room for my private meeting with Dr. Cobbler that was dubbed 'extremely urgent' according to the email subject line.

I quickly reach the conference room and open the door, Dr. Cobbler stopping mid conversation with a man and woman police officer on either side of him, and looking up at me with his large, T-Rex eyes.

"John, you're here." Dr. Cobbler says coolly.

Tucker appears abruptly behind me. "I'm sorry, doctor! I told him that he couldn't come back here."

Dr. Cobbler just stares at Tucker with a blank expression on his face. "Why did you tell him not to come back here?"

"Because he's not authorized." Tucker says.

Dr. Cobbler just shakes his head and beckons me inside. "Thank you Tucker, we're okay from here."

The security guard nods and steps back into the hallway, letting the door close behind him.

I take a seat across from the doctor and his two police companions at the end of our long white conference table.

"As you've heard, we had a break in a few days ago." Dr. Cobbler tells me.

I nod, my heart skipping a beat. "I've heard."

"As far as we know, the only thing that has gone missing is a single hard drive's worth of security footage. However, it appears that the helicopter was also tampering in one of our highest security clearance labs." Dr. Cobbler explains.

"Helicopter?" I ask. "How do you know it was a helicopter?"

The doctor slides an assortment of black and white photos across the table towards me and as I look down that them my breath catches in my throat.

"The stolen drive contained footage from all of the indoor cameras, however, the outdoor cameras remained functional and we captured these photos of the suspect." The doctor explains. "Have you ever seen this helicopter?"

I try my best to act as though I've got nothing to conceal, spreading the security camera screenshots out in front of me and carefully looking over every one. The photos are shockingly high resolution, revealing every detail of my appearance as Chibs Pratt.

"No, I've never seen him before." I tell the dinosaur.

Dr. Cobbler nods silently for a moment, then leans back into his chair and let's the man next to him take over.

"I'm Detective Kellogg, with the FBI." The handsome older man tells me. "And this is my partner, Detective Peek."

"Nice to meet you." I say.

"We've got a few questions for you in regards to the break in, and this living object, along with your whereabouts on the day in question." Detective Kellogg continues.

"You're not under arrest." Detective Peek informs me, chiming in. "So you're not required to talk to us, but your help is appreciated. This is a matter of high government security."

I nod. "I'm fine with talking to you, it's not a problem. I'm just trying to help."

"Good." Kellogg tells me. "Then maybe you can help clarify a few things for me; first off, tell us where you went after leaving the security meeting in this room on the day of the break in."

"Well." I start, my brain immediately kicking into high gear, ready for anything. "I left to get my keycard upgraded for the next security system, but I couldn't find the lab."

"How long have you been working here?" Detective Kellogg asks skeptically. "You just forgot where the lab was?"

"I think Doctor Cobbler told me the wrong one." I explain. "It was a crazy day here."

"He told you the wrong lab?" Detective Kellogg questions. "And what was the wrong lab that he told you?"

I hesitate for a moment. "I don't remember."

The detective nods for a moment and then writes something down. I can plainly tell that he doesn't buy my story.

"So what happened after that?" The detective asks, looking up at me.

"I went looking for the lab and I figure I must have gotten lost. I started to get a headache and wasn't feeling very well after that, though, so I just went home." I explain.

"You went home, and you didn't feel the need to mention that to anyone? To your boss?" The detective pushes even further.

"No." I say, flatly. "I just went home, I was too sick."

The officer seems to be deep in thought regarding my answer, and I can't tell if it's because he believes me or because he knows something that I don't.

"That's interesting." Detective Kellogg says. "What exit did you leave from?"

I pause and think about this for a moment. "The front door, I didn't see anything happening out back."

Kellogg nods again. "The crazy thing is, there are security cameras on the front door." He says. "And the back door, too. In fact, every entrance of this facility has a security camera fixed right there on it."

"Sometimes two." Detective Peek adds.

"Sometimes two." Kellogg confirms. "Me and Detective Peek here must have watched hours and hours of footage, but for the life of us, we can't find any video of you leaving this building after work."

My heart is nearly pounding out of my chest at this point, beads of sweat surfacing across my forehead despite my best efforts to stay calm. If I don't get myself under control, and fast, the nanobots will corrupt and I'll start drifting apart right here in front of them.

"It looks like your car has been parked in the lot for a few days, too." Says Detective Peek. "That's a little strange, wouldn't you say?"

I sit in silence for a moment, not sure if this is a rhetorical question or not.

"Wouldn't you say, John Hams?" Kellogg asks again.

"It's pretty strange." I tell them.

"Care to explain?" Kellogg prods.

My gaze moves tensely between Doctor Cobbler and the two detectives, wondering if I should give up right here and now. I have no reasonable answer for them, nothing that could make sense of any of this. However, they also don't seem to have any answers for themselves. This entire situation may be utterly bizarre, but since when has being bizarre been a crime?

"I..." My voice shakes as I try desperately to come up with something. "I guess you should check the tapes again."

"We've checked them plenty." Detective Kellogg says. "And it still doesn't add up."

Suddenly, a stroke of brilliance hits me so hard that it almost knocks me over backwards in my chair. Visions of the man and woman who installed the security system flow into my head, particularly the man who started crying over the rats and had to leave while covering his face.

"Did you see anyone with their coat over their head?" I ask.

The two detectives look at each other, slightly concerned about the possible curve ball I've thrown their way, and more than a little confused.

"I don't think so." Kellogg tells me, and then asks Detective Peek.

"Did we see anyone with a jacket over their head?"

"I don't know." Peek answers. "I'd have to go back and check the tapes."

"Well, that was me." I respond. "I went to get my keycard fixed but slipped on some of the security equipment that was sitting out in the hallway, waiting to be installed."

Doctor Cobbler suddenly looks terrified, probably sensing a potential lawsuit in his future.

"It happened at the top of the stairs that lead down to level two, and I fell down them." I explain. "Shook me up so bad that I had to call a friend to come pick me up, that's why my car is still here. I was crying, and embarrassed. I didn't want anyone to see me like that so I changed into some new clothes and then rushed out the door with a jacket over my head."

Kellogg eyes me suspiciously. "Why'd you change your clothes?"

"It was a bad fall." I tell him. "My shirt was ripped and bloody, so I changed into something I had lying around in my office.

"You don't look too scarred up." Detective Peek says with a laugh. "You look just fine."

I stand up from my chair and turn away from them, willing the nanobots to create a massive swath of warped, distorted tissue across my back as I pull up my shirt. The group lets out an audible gasp, and when I turn back to face them, Doctor Cobbler looks white as a sheet.

"Is that everything?" I ask.

I can tell that none of them buy it, the room tense with a heavy skepticism, but that this point they're really nothing that they can say or do about it. I turn and start to head for the door when suddenly Doctor Cobbler stops me.

"John Hams." The dinosaur doctor says. "I think you should stay home the rest of the week while we sort this out, take some time off. It's all paid, I just think it would be best if you weren't here in the building."

Having barely just gotten out of the conference room without handcuffs around my wrists, I'm in no position to protest. Instead, I nod in affirmation.

"We'll check the tapes again and get back to you." Detective Kellogg says.

On the way home from the lab I call Yorb on my car phone, but he doesn't answer. Pangs of guilt surge through me, having no idea what kind of turmoil this incredible man's life could be in right now simply because of my actions the other night.   I'll try again later.

In the meantime, with all of this shape shifting nanobot drama going on, I haven't had time to take care of any monotonous, daily chores at all. I've got packages to take to the post office, groceries to buy, and bills to pay; and no amount of experimental technology is going to change that,

It's a long day, and by the time I get home I'm absolutely exhausted, flopping down onto the couch and almost immediately drifting off into a state of deep thought.

My thoughts, however, are very specific.

Finally, a moment to relax and all that runs through my head are powerful cravings to fuck. I think back to the way that Yorb felt inside of my butt, the incredible sensation of his muscular body pulsing against mine.

I reach down and let my hand slip under the waistband of my pants and underwear, my fingers gently wrapping themselves around my engorged cock.

A sharp but pleasant chill runs down my spine as I let out a long, satisfied sigh and push farther back into the couch cushions.

With my other hand I reach over and grab my phone, then dial Yorb's number for the second time today, waiting patiently while it rings over and over against and then eventually goes to voicemail. I hang up and quickly sent him a text that simply reads, 'It's John Hams. Call me.'

Touching myself feels incredible, I must admit, especially since I had even been abstaining from this kind of self-love for both years, as well.

However, there is only so much satisfaction one can get while touching themselves after a night of such incredible sex. I've tasted the sweetness and now I'm trying to revert to a sex life without sugar, magic or mystery. I know deep down that I shouldn't be having any of this at all, but the idea of returning to complete abstinence at this point is ridiculous. There is an aching fire that burns deep within me, and now there's no way of putting it out.

I stop the movements of my hand across my shaft, a fierce internal battle waging within my mind. The conflict doesn't last long, though.

Moments later, I stand abruptly and head for the door, my body morphing and changing as I walk and, by the time I reach the hallway of my apartment complex, I've already transformed into Chibs Pratt, the hot, gay, helicopter.

8 BAR SCENE BLUES

This bar, like all the others in our lives, is nothing more than a marketplace. We enter and peruse the selection, the beautiful displays that have been laid out before us, and then eventually we make an offer.

Often the offer is too low, the man's show of power too meek for the other to take notice. After all, there's a whole room of other buyers just waiting to pounce and throw their hat into the ring. Sometimes a guy takes a little longer than expected to show his true worth, revealing it through witty conversation or, more to the point, by dropping a significant amount of money on expensive drinks. Eventually, if the target is impressed, the two of them will leave together, mutually satisfied with the transaction.

It's a dance that's been played out over and over again for thousands of years, in different places with different people, even different species, but for the most part the steps of love and lust are always the same, and they're hardwired within us.

I haven't personally witnessed this type of interaction in years, but suddenly being thrust back into it like this is just as thrilling as the very first time.

Of course, my scientific, analytical nature makes it hard to just go with the flow and enjoy myself, but for me this kind of analysis is all part of the fun. I feel as though I'm the host of my very own nature show, about the mating habits of human beings.

However, tonight something feels wrong. As a lone helicopter posted up on the bar with a drink in my hand (non-alcoholic mind you, I'm not sure how beer or spirits will react with the nanobot programming), I recall men being much quicker to swarm in and take their shots at me.

Tonight, I remain alone, watching as the rest of the tavern pairs off with one another in their timeless mating ritual. Why is it so hard for a living vehicle like me to get laid around here? I'm ten times hotter than I ever was when I had been my average, frumpy self, but now that I've become Chibs Pratt, the men should be flocking. Women too; and why not?

Suddenly, it hits me. Maybe that's exactly the problem, maybe I'm too hot to approach?

I stand up from my stool at the bar and down the rest of my drink, then head towards a table of men in one of the dark corners of the room. There are three of them, all viciously sexy in a rugged, biker kind of way. Without a word I slide into the booth next to them, causing the trio to stop mid conversation and look me over in a mixture of confusion and thankful excitement.

"Well hello there." One of them says. "How are you doing tonight, chopper?"

I smile. "I'm alright. How are you boys doing?"

"Good, good." The man says with a nod. "I'm Pete, and these two knuckleheads are Jim and Kyle."

The men flash me slightly uncomfortable smiles, which is a little funny given their ruthless biker demeanor. Even men this rugged can't completely keep their cool in front of a helicopter this beautiful.

"I'm Chibs." I say warmly.

"That's a sexy name, dude." Jim tells me, and I respond with a wink.

"Thank you. You three looking to get into some trouble tonight?" I ask the table.

The guys look back and forth between one another, as if mutually trying to decide if I'm serious or not. "What do you mean by that?" Pete asks. "You're not a helicopter hooker are you?"

"No." I roll my eyes. "Jesus, do I have to spell it out for you? Do you want to fuck me?"

Pete's jaw drops. "Are you…" He stammers. "Are you serious?"

"I'm not going to ask again." I tell them.

The men all nod in unison and I stand up from the booth, motioning for them to follow me.

My heart is nearly pounding out of my chest as we exit the bar together. Never in my life have I imagined doing something this wild, not that this particular opportunity had ever been thrown my way, regardless. I'm doubtful that a week ago, in my previous, nanobot free life, I would have even wanted such a thing, but having a new identity is a powerful thing.

Not only does my new appearance as Chibs Pratt give me more confidence than I ever had, but the lack of consequences is intoxicating. It's the perfect way to release all of these years of pent up sexual energy, and if there's no hot raptors around, then these human men will just have to do.

But, as I lead the men around the corner to a darkened alley behind the bar, the truth of just how out of control I've managed to get in the span of these few days hits me hard. A back alley gangbang is not exactly where I expected to end up when I decided to use Chibs Pratt to seduce Yorb, but at this point he's taken on a life of his own and I'm just along for the ride.

"Holy shit." Pete says as we find our place in the shadows. "Are you for real?"

"No." I tell him, more truthful than he could ever understand, then kiss the man passionately on the lips.

I tremble as he runs his hands up and down my exceptionally built cockpit, happily taking in every toned inch of my metal body. One of the other men steps up behind me and starts to kiss me on tail boom, exploring me with his hands as well. I let out as satisfied groan as the guy overwhelm me with their powerful arms pushing my huge helicopter body up against the alley wall.

"Fuck." Is all that I can manage to say, rock hard as they get to work beneath my hull, stroking my huge, aching cock.

I can hear the jingling of unbuckled belts as the men unsheathe their cocks, and I grasp the air for them frantically, eventually snatching one in each blade and getting to work in the darkness as I stroke them off.

The guys reel with satisfaction as I touch them with my metallic blades, eyes closed and bodies quaking. Their cocks are enormous and hard as rocks within my grip, which quickens with every stroke. Soon enough, I'm beating them off ferociously, giving the guys everything I've got as I work their throbbing shafts.

I'm too overwhelmingly horny to think, completely consumed by my arousal. Consequences be damned, I want these men to take me any way that they'd like.   Somewhere deep down inside, a voice is yelling for me to stop, but it's too faint and at this point I'm not really interested in listening.

Driven mad with lust, I immediately take Pete into my helicopter mouth, swallowing him down as far as I can and them rapidly bobbing my head across his shaft.

Meanwhile, I continue to pump my hands along the cocks of the guys on either side of me, expertly satisfying all three of them at once.

Eventually, I begin to move back and forth between their shafts, giving each of the three men equal time between my lips as they pound away at my handsome mechanical face. I'm completely cock crazed at this point, losing track of which one is which as I shove their rods down my throat, sometimes two at a time.

I'm so lost in the mayhem that I can barely hear my phone ringing within my cockpit, but the second that I do I pull the men's cocks out of my mouth and snap back to reality.

I reach in with a blade, then take out my phone and see Yorb's name flashing across the screen.

"Sorry guys." I say, swiveling abruptly and pushing past them. "I've gotta take this."

The men start to protest but I'm already walking back out of the alley towards the main street.

"Hello?" I answer. "Yorb?"

His voice seems lifeless and brooding as it returns to me through the earpiece. "Hey John. Where are you?"

I look up at the sign that hangs above the bar, having already forgotten where I was. "The Oakwood Tavern." I tell him.

"I'm pretty close." Yorb tells me, straight to the point. "Can I come get you?"

My heart flutters a bit as he said this, a brief moment of love in the thick sea of lust that my life has quickly become. "Yes." I answer. "Please."

"Be there in a few minutes." Yorb tells me, then hangs up the phone to leave me standing here alone out on the empty street corner.

I take in a deep breath, trying to center myself amid all of this raging emotional confusion. What am I doing here? The addition of Yorb back into my life, even in such a small way, immediately reminds me of what I truly want, and fucking three guys in the back alley isn't it.

"Hey!" Comes a voice from behind me, I turn around and see Pete staggering back out from the darkness, struggling to tighten his belt. "What the fuck?"

"Sorry bud." I tell him. "I've gotta run."

A look of drunken anger crosses his face, shocked that I could talk to him so bluntly like this. "You're just gonna leave us out to dry like that?" Pete questions, his friends stepping up behind him.

"It's my blowjob to give." I laugh. "So it's also my blowjob to take away."

The group of us stand in silence for a moment, staring each other down. It suddenly occurs to me that I'm all alone out here, the night air quiet and not another soul in sight. The nearest person who would care if I called out is the bouncer at The Oakwood, but he's sitting inside by the door and the door is currently shut.

The trio of bikers must be thinking the same thing, because they seem to immediately realize that they don't have much time to act, springing into action as they rush me abruptly.

I try to scream but Pete is quick to cover my mouth as the others lift me off of my feet and pull me back into the darkness of the ally, trying desperately to rotate my blades and force them off of me.

Had I never broken my celibacy this wouldn't have happened, I think to myself, then try my best to push those thoughts out of my head. It's not my fault, I'm the victim here. These men are the ones who are to blame, not me.

Pete, Jim and Kyle have me pinned down now, my rotor held in place and my skids pressed hard onto the hard cement as Kyle positions himself in front of me with his huge cock.

In my panic, I can feel the nanobots within me becoming violently unstable, stretching and pulling my helicopter body into small, but strange contortions. I can't even begin to try and collect myself, rendered helpless by all of the chaos that swirls around me as I try to push the men away. For a split second I consider changing myself into something extreme and terrifying to frighten them, but my brain is so scattered and hectic that I'm concerned I won't be able to focus enough on the transformation, and end up like one of those poor, contorted, lab rat corpses.

Still, without any other options, I have to try something.

Focusing all of the mental energy that I have left, I try desperately to change back into a human. No dice.

I try once again, hoping that the abrupt physical shift may scare the men off. I focus all of my mental energy on assuming my previous human shape.

This time it works, but somehow the men surrounding me barely seem to notice. I've returned to my original form, John Hams, but the guys are too drunk to tell the difference.

There's no way out of this, I quickly realize, utterly helpless.

Suddenly, there's a loud crack as Kyle flies off of me, and a second once as his head hits the pavement, knocking him unconscious. I look up to see Yorb standing over me and I'm immediately consumed by an awesome wave of relief.

There's no time for pleasantries however, because the next thing I know Pete and Jim are jumping to their feet and taking swings at my handsome stegosaurus hero. They both miss in their drunken stupor, and Yorb easily dispatches with Jim by giving him two swift claws to the head and dropping him instantly.

I quickly notice how fluid Yorb's movements are, as if he's running through a delicate piece of choreography that's been rehearsed for years. His wounds and broken bones from earlier years don't seem to slow him down at all.

Suddenly, I catch a glimpse of metal flashing in the dim light of the ally as Pete pulls a switchblade from his pocket.

"Look out!" I shriek.

Pete jabs at Yorb, who deftly moves out of the way and delivers a hard, stegosaurus head butt to Pete's stomach. Unfortunately, though, this allows Pete inside Yorb's defenses. Upon the biker's second jab with the knife he strikes Yorb in the side, causing the wounded dinosaur to let out a painful cry and stumble backwards as Pete advances upon him.

Painfully aware of where this is headed, I immediately spring to my feet and grab a thick plank of wood that's been leaned up against the alley wall. I swing it as hard as I can at the back of Pete's skull and with a deafening crack he goes down, immediately crumpling up into a ball on the ground.

I throw my arms around Yorb, who's happy to see me but winces in pain as our bodies meet.

"You're hurt." I say, pulling back and looking down at the blood that oozes from beneath his shirt.

Yorb laughs. "Can't a dinosaur go a day without getting stabbed in a fucking back alley?"

"Come on." I say, helping him out of the alleyway and away from the groaning men, who remain in various stages of consciousness on the hard cement ground. "You need help."

I pull out my phone as we walk and dial nine-one-one.

9 VIVA LAS VEGAS

After finishing our brief statements for the police, Yorb and I sit quietly on the back steps of the ambulance who's crew, thankfully, managed to fix him up quite swiftly and easily. The stabbing missed anything vital by a long shot, bouncing off a rib bone near the surface of Yorb's chest.

The two of us are exhausted but happy to be sitting together, and I can tell the feeling is mutual as Yorb wraps his arm around me and pulls me as close as possible, without putting too much pressure on his carefully bandaged wound.

I lean my head against the handsome beast's broad shoulder and take in his now familiar, reptilian scent.

"I'm glad you called me." I tell Yorb.

"I'm glad I got here when I did." He says, staring off into space. The two of us have gone through the wringer over the last few days, which I suppose is to be expected as far as relapsing goes.

"I need a break." I finally say.

Yorb chuckles to himself. "You're telling me. It's been a hard couple of days."

I know all too well what he means, and I instantly regret putting him through all of this. Everything bad that has happened since we met has been my fault, a series of events brought on by my lust, envy, and a seemingly endless string of bad decisions. Of course, he also has no idea that I'm really the helicopter who has been systematically destroying his life.

"I don't know what to do with myself." I tell Yorb, my voice cracking as I struggle to hold back my tears. "I feel like I'm losing my mind. I'm turning into someone else and I'm afraid that I can't stop it."

Yorb pulls me even closer to him and looks down, flatly ignoring the pain from his fresh wound. "What happened?"

I know that I can't tell him everything, that at this point it's just too crazy and, frankly, too dangerous to let anyone else know what a powerful, and destructive, person I've become. "I've relapsed." I tell him, the most I'm willing to admit just yet.

"Is that why you're out tonight?" Yorb asks.

It burns my soul to consider what he'll think of me after I tell him, but I know how important it is to take inventory of my own mistakes. "Yes." I admit.

Yorb is silent for a moment, and then opens himself up to me, as well. "I've relapsed too. I need help but I can't go back to the group."

"Trouble with Forbok?" I ask, already knowing the answer to my own question.

Yorb nods. "We're not together any longer."

"Oh." I say, struggling to sound surprised. "I'm sorry to hear that."

We watch as Pete is taken away in handcuffs, pushing back against the police officers are they force him down into the back of their cruiser. He's spitting and swearing, completely out of control.

I lower my head in shame.

"Why did you call me tonight?" I ask Yorb.

He let's out a sigh. "I don't know. I mean, I guess I know why, but it sounds stupid."

"Try me." I tell him.

Yorb pulls his coin out of his pocket and starts flipping it. "You want to know the secret of being a good gambler?" He asks.

"What's that?"

"Not believing in anything. No god, no ghosts, no magic… but especially no luck."

"But you talk about luck all the time." I counter. "Or risk, at least."

"And there's the difference." He says with a chuckle. "It's fun to think about, to pretend that there are these forces at work outside of ourselves pulling all the strings; The magic dice that can turn it all around when you're down and out. It makes for great stories, but it's not real."

"Doesn't sound like much fun to me." I tell him. "What a sad world."

"Fair enough." Yorb says. "But, if you want to make money playing cards or shooting dice, the first thing you need to do is throw away everything you know about luck and start thinking about strategy."

"Okay," I answer. "I get that, but what does this have to do with you calling me?"

"That night at the diner." Yorb says. "When we were talking. I felt this connection and, honestly, I don't understand it. I don't believe in magic, but there's magic in the air when we're together."

Again the tears start welling up in my eyes, but instead of sadness and disappointment, they represent a welcome relief. "I felt it too." I tell him.

"Maybe magic *is* real." Yorb says. "Maybe love is real."

A slow smile creeps across my face, realizing that something good is finally blooming in the horrific wreckage of my life.

We're silent for a moment before Yorb suddenly lets out a loud laugh at his own internal joke.

"What was that about?" I ask him.

"I need to get my shit together." He tells me. "Look at me."

"Me too. Oh my god, me too." I start laughing with him, unable to do anything else in the face of my own absurdly devastating downfall. "So what's the plan? What do we do?" I ask the handsome dinosaur.

"Skip town. Dry out for a bit." Yorb tells me.

As good as that sounds, being alone with this man who I'm so viciously attracted to might not be the best thing for my sexual sobriety. Of course, if there's one thing that Forbok was able to teach me, it's that my plight is not about abstaining from sex, it's about abstaining from random, meaningless sex.

It may be newly blossoming, but there's no way that what Yorb and I have going on between us is meaningless.

"It sounds dangerous." I tell him. "Where would we go?"

"Vegas." Yorb informs me, causing me to scoff loudly.

"Even more dangerous! You honestly think we should get clean and figure our shit out in sin city?" I laugh.

Yorb shrugs. "What better way to fight a lurking monster than to take it head on?"

The guy has a strange, maniacal logic to him, I'll give him that.

"Besides." Yorb continues. "It's not like I'm lacking in finances, but I've got so many comps left over from my years throwing money around in that town, I could probably live in Las Vegas free of charge for a decade."

"Vegas it is." I tell him. "When do we leave?"

Yorb thinks about this a moment. "Do you need to call in to your work?" He asks.

"No." I shake my head. "I think they fired me. I'm not really sure."

Yorb starts to laugh again, so hard this time that he's forced to release me from his grip and clutch his side, in an attempt to quell the pain. "Your life really is falling apart!" He jokes.

I try to stifle my grin but I can't. "So when do we leave?" I ask again.

Yorb stands up from his seat on the edge of the ambulance. "Right now."

I sleep the entire way as Yorb drives through the night, flying across the open desert between California and Nevada like a bat out of hell. In some ways, a bat out of hell is exactly what we're hoping for, and escape from the jaws of vice before it's too late. Of course, most people would argue that Vegas is even more of a hellish urban landscape than Los Angeles, but Yorb assures me that, with his connections, we'll be finding ourselves in a situation that's far from sinful.

I try not to project too far into the future, but in my deep drifting sleep I let my thoughts wander. Maybe we could even find real, true love.

When I awaken we've arrived at the front entrance of a towering, behemoth-of-a-hotel and casino. It's around one thirty in the morning.

"We're here." Yorb says. "Don't worry, you can go right up into the room and go to bed. I'll handle everything down here."

I nod at Yorb in a tired haze and climb out of his flamboyant sports car, then look up at the sparking letters that stand before me in flickering neon yellow, 'The Keen Dangler Casino'.

I've heard about this place but never stayed here, the facilities resting several income brackets out of my price range.

Almost immediately, someone approaches me and takes my bag out of my hands, while another person hands me a room key.

"Already?" I ask, dumbfounded. "That was quick."

"They know me here." Yorb answers, just head on up, I'm gonna take care of a few things. You can have the room near the balcony.

Too exhausted for anything other than getting into the nearest comfy bed possible, I take my room key and stagger through the giant front doors of the casino, immediately met by a barrage of loud ringing and flashing lights. The air is sweet and perks me up almost immediately, as if pumped in and circulated with the express intent of exciting my senses.

Still, this madness is no match for my devastating fatigue, and I immediately head for the nearest elevator. Maybe Yorb is right about heading for the heart of the monster and facing our vice head on, because the last thing I want to do right now is make bad choices.

The elevator ride is quick, and almost immediately I find myself transported to an entirely different space, more akin to an ultra modern spa. There is a small hallway with only two doors, one on either side.

I use my room key and push the door open, revealing the most gorgeous hotel suite that I've ever seen. The main living quarters are the size of middle class families entire home, with a giant winding staircase jutting up through the middle like a corkscrew. Behind it lies a beautiful view of the Las Vegas strip, complete with a wrap around deck and an infinity hot tub that appears to cascade endlessly over the edge.

I take it all in for a few moments and then I cross over towards a door located off to the side of the balcony, which I can only assume is my room. Sure enough, when I open it up there is a beautiful king sized bed waiting for me. I let out a glorious sigh of relief and then immediately strip down, climb in, and pull the covers up tight.

As I drift off to sleep I imagine Yorb arriving at the suite and, despite our best efforts to take things slow, climbing into bed with me. I picture him kissing me all over with his sweet dinosaur lips, touching my body in ways that only someone desperately and passionately in love can. Nothing fake, and nothing held back.

I know that Yorb and me can figure all of this craziness out here in Las Vegas; together.

"What the fuck?" Is the first think that I hear, jolting me suddenly out of my pleasant slumber. I open my eyes to see Yorb standing in the doorway of my room, the morning sun shining beams of glorious light through my window.

"What is it?" I mumble, "What's happening?"

It's only then that I notice there are two other figures in bed with me, curled up on either side. I look down to see a man and a woman who, as far as I can tell, are completely naked.

"Oh my god!" I say, sitting upright abruptly and waking my two sleeping partners.

Yorb's expression is one of utter horror and complete disappointment, stunned and silent as my apparent lovers from the night before stir under the blankets.

The woman next to me snuggles close and sleepily opens her eyes, but when she sees me she recoils in shock. "Whoa! What the fuck?"

Suddenly, the man is awake, as well, and the entire room is thrown into a state of total chaos with me at the dead center.

Yorb just shakes his head and leaves, heading out of our room and, very likely, out of my life.

"Yorb! Wait!" I shout, but the confused bickering of the couple on either side of me drowns out the sound of my cries.

10 BLACK OUT

"Who are you?" The woman keeps shouting at me. "Where's Chibs the helicopter?"

The man is trying to get her to calm down but it's not working and their fighting is giving me a splitting headache.

Finally, I just can't take it anymore, climbing out of bed and pulling on my clothes. "I'm sorry but the two of you need to leave right now." I tell them.

The man follows suit behind me, collecting several articles of his clothing that have been scattered around the room.

My brain is throbbing deep within my skull, a splitting ache that could only have come from a night of severe drinking. I try my best to remember something, anything, about what occurred just hours before and how I ended up here dealing with the aftermath of an apparent threesome.

"Come on, let's go back to the room, Mary." The man urges. "He was nice enough to let us stay in her suite last night, but we need to go now."

"He was?!" The woman yells, completely losing her cool. "Who the fuck is he? Where's Chibs?"

It suddenly hits me what has happened, and the realization nearly causes me to buckle at the knees and collapse out of sheer, unbridled frustration. Chibs Pratt took our body for a spin last night, causing me to relapse whether I wanted it or not. He's growing stronger and stronger every day, and now he doesn't even need to ask my permission, apparently.

"I'm sorry." I say, trying to calm the woman down. "I know this seems weird, but I'm Chibs."

Mary scoffs. "I was drunk, but I wasn't that drunk."

"I swear to you, I'm Chibs." I assure her. "But it doesn't matter anyway, you both need to leave."

As I say the this man crosses the room over to Mary and tries to take her by the arm, but she's having none of it, and immediately the woman takes a swing at him. She misses feebly. It suddenly occurs to me that it's early enough for this chick to probably still be drunk.

"What did you do with Chibs?" Mary starts to shriek.

"Calm down!" I tell her. "I'm Chibs!"

"No you're not!" The woman cries. "Where is he?"

Frustrated, and without anything else to think of doing, I suddenly will myself into the helicopter transformation, my body morphing and shifting into this gorgeous black aircraft right before the couple's very eyes.

The room immediately gets quiet as the two of them watch me, their voices dropping and their faces turning from anger to awe and then, moments later, fear.

"I'm sorry." The woman says, her eyes transfixed on me as she grabs her clothes from the floor and, not even bothering to but them on, makes her way out the door.

"Don't be sorry." Chibs says. "How about another round before you go?"

I suddenly freeze, realizing that, although the words may have come from somewhere deep within my body, they were not my own.

"I don't think so." Says the man. The couple make their way out into the living room, clearly disturbed after witnessing my transformation, and when they are far enough away they turn and heard straight for the door, leaving without another word or even a look back over their shoulders.

"What did you do?" I shout at Chibs.

"Took what I wanted." The helicopter says.

I fully understand that Chibs is just me standing here in the middle of the room and talking to myself, but for the moment that's real enough of a chopper to yell at.

"We can't do this anymore, it's over!" I tell him as firmly as I can.

The helicopter scoffs. "Please. I'm the one who's calling the shots now."

Immediately, I attempt to transform myself back into my original state, but the change simply won't occur no matter how desperately I want it do.

"Fuck." I say.

Chibs laughs. "Exactly, I'd love a good fuck right about now."

"Please, no." I beg. "We need to go find Yorb and tell him everything."

"Yorb?" Chibs says in a mocking tone. "Why settle for one billionaire dinosaur when you could have them all?"

I pause for a moment, grappling with the reality of what I'm about to say. "Because, I love him."

"Love is for suckers." Chibs tells me with my own mouth. "Let's have some fun."

"The last time you wanted to have fun you got us in a lot of trouble." I tell him. "Yorb got stabbed."

"That's only because you tried to stop me." The chopper says. "I suggest you don't try it again."

I try to respond but suddenly I find myself unable to, locked out from using my own mouth. I now feel like I'm a passenger in my own body, traveling along in the head of a living object who started in my imagination and now lives and breathes like I do. Chibs Pratt is the commander of the ship now, a nightmare in the metal.

Suddenly, I'm heading for the door, then out into the hallway and down the elevator to the casino floor. Once again, I find myself staring at my own reflection in the elevator door, the unfamiliar cockpit and rotor of Chibs Pratt staring back at me. Granted, it's a beautiful body, but it's not my own, and now the sight of him fills me with utter dread. Things have already gone way too far and now I'm free falling, unable to stop myself no matter how hard I try.

As the elevator door opens I want nothing more than to go look for Yorb, to find him and explain everything, but that's not at all what happens.

Instead, I turn and head deep into the rows and rows of slot machines, ringing and clattering all around me as people hit or miss their jackpots over and over again. Flashing lights guide my way, helping me navigate the isles as I scan the chairs for a suitable target.

It's not long before I find him, a handsome older man with salt and pepper hair who's wearing a nicely cut suit. He doesn't look like he belongs in this end of the casino, and is probably killing time while he waits for someone upstairs to meet up with him. Lucky for me, I get there first.

"Hey there." I say, sitting down at the machine next to the man.

He turns to me and smiles, immediately taken by my hulls smoldering craftsmanship, from my windshield to the abs down below. The man extends his hand and I take it in one of my blades. "I'm Mark." He says. "Nice to meet you."

"Chibs Pratt." I tell him.

"And where are you from, Chibs?" Mark asks.

"Los Angeles." I respond. "But you don't really give a fuck about that do you? Be honest."

Mark laughs uncomfortably. "Of course I do!"

"No." I shake my head. "But it's your lucky day, because I don't care either. You know what I do care about, though?"

Mark shakes his head, simultaneous baffled and entertained by my strange behavior. "I care about getting fucked up this tight little helicopter ass." I tell him.

Marks eyes go wide and he immediately looks over either shoulder, checking to see if anyone else heard my outrageous comment.

"Think you could help me with that?" I ask.

"You're sure blunt." Mark says. I can tell that he's more than a little interested, if nothing else, by the quickly hardening cock that grows within the finely woven fabric of his suit pants.

"Cut it with the small talk." I demand. "Are you interested in helping me out?"

"Yeah, but…" Mark starts. I immediately cut him off, grabbing him by the tie and pulling him to his feet as I stand and make a b-line for the nearest restroom.

I push open the door of the men's room, which is occupied by three or four other guys already, and drag Mark into one of the stalls, slamming the door behind us.

Wasting no time, I tear off Mark's jacket and pull his shirt up over his head, then kiss him deeply on the mouth. There is barley enough room for a helicopter and a human to fit inside of here, but we make it work.

Mark's muscular body feels incredible on my cold metal frame. I push the man back against the wall of the stall and continue to make out with him, running my blades softly and carefully across his toned abs and unbuckling his belt but, before I can do anything else, Mark turns the tables and pushes me down onto the toilet seat, where I sit and look up at him with hungry, lustful eyes.

Seconds later, Mark in kneeling before me, crawling onto the floor and looking up at my engorged cock that hangs down below my hull. Mark waists no time, swallowing my thickness into his hungry, waiting mouth.

I let out a gentle moan as he pleasures me, closing my eyes and leaning my tail boom back against the hard bathroom wall behind me.

"Oh fuck." I moan. "Keep going, just like that."

I manage to get one of my landing skids up and locked into a bar on one side of the stall, giving Mark even more room to maneuver as he bobs his head up and down across my shaft. His technique is incredible, immediately sending chills of pleasure up and down my spine while the handsome, older man works his magic.

From the small crack at the bottom of the stall I can see the shadows of other guys who have drawn closer to the action, brought on by the passionate sounds of a hunky young helicopter in heat.

"Looks like we've got an audience." I say, nodding towards the stall door. "Better not disappoint them."

This kicks mark into overdrive, and the next thing I know he's climbing back onto his knees and unsheathing his absolutely enormous cock. He climbs around to the side of me and then places his shaft up against the aching entrance of my fuel hole, teasing me for a moment, and then he pushes forward, impaling me onto his thick rod.

I let out a gasp as Mark enters me, not entirely ready for his substantial size. Fortunately for me, though, Mark knows what he's doing and soon enough I find myself in the troughs of pleasure, the man slowly but firmly pumping in and out of my body.

Overwhelmed by lust, I grab Mark by the hips and pull him towards me with more and more force every time until eventually he's slamming into me as hard as he can, rocking the stall loudly with every thrust against my helicopter butthole as he gains speed.

Outside, one of the other men makes a muffled comment and the rest of them suddenly burst out laughing, excited by the decadent encounter that they've randomly found themselves an audible witness to.

I can feel myself slowly start to edge towards orgasm. I'm not ready to cum yet, though, so, biting my lip playfully, I eventually push Mark back and sit up.

"How about we put on a little show?" I coo.

Without hesitation I kick open the stall door with one foot, revealing Mark and myself to the excited crowd of onlookers. The men immediately burst into a chorus of catcalls as I stand up and turn around, bending over with my blades gripping tightly onto the back of the toilet. I give my tail boom a playful wiggle for them and then look back at Mark with a wink and a nod. He knows exactly what I want.

The next thing I know, Mark is aligning the head of his cock with the taut rim of my asshole, pushing gently against the clenched muscle. I expertly use the nanobots to relax myself, easing the tension as Mark slips inside with a satisfied groan.

Abruptly, I let out a yelp of my own, a strange mixture of pleasure and slight aching discomfort as Mark slips deeper and deeper, and then comes to a stop at the hilt of his massive shaft. Now completely within my depths, the man gives my tail boom a hard smack and I laugh, his dominance filling me with another quick surge of mischievous gay arousal.

The next thing I know, Mark is pumping my fuel hole with the entire length of his huge member, egged on by excited shouts from the other men. They crane around the edge of the stall to get a look at me, cheering and hollering. Most of them have their cocks out now and are beating them furiously.

As Mark speeds up, I reach down and start to beat off my cock, helping myself along as I drift closer and closer to an inevitable, and powerful, orgasm.

"Oh my god, don't stop!" I scream, my voice strange an unfamiliar as it exits through Chibs Pratt's helicopter vocal cords. "Keep slamming me until I cum!"

I can feel the familiar, warm sensation begin to blossom within my body, creeping its way down my arms in legs as I tremble and shake. My knees are locked, everything within me stretched tight against the oncoming convulsions and then suddenly a tidal wave of prostate pleasure hits me, releasing all of the tension at once. I'm screaming in ecstasy, completely losing control of myself as my muscles contract in a series of blissful spasms. A powerful blast of semen ejects hard from the head of my cock.

The sensation overwhelms me and I give into it completely, letting myself feel it all as Mark continues to hammer away behind me. He's shaking as well, and then suddenly proceeds to blast a massive payload of semen up into my asshole. I can feel his cock twitch hard with every injection, until finally there is nothing left within him and Mark pulls out of me, exhausted.

The group of guys watching us cheers loudly.

I immediately start to collect my clothing, pulling it back on as I stumble out of the restroom in a fucked-silly daze. I'm filled with a swirling cocktail of emotions that pulls me this way and that but, most of all, what I want is to get away from all this.

I'm satisfied, but in my satisfaction I see an escape from Chibs, a moment to keep my compulsion repressed just enough to reclaim my sanity.

Quickly, I duck into an empty row of slot machines, and then desperately will myself to transform back into John Hams. As I do, I watch a crew of five security guards run into the men's room, but by the time they come out looking for Mr. Pratt, he's nowhere to be found.

There's no time to celebrate, however.

As I walk through the casino looking for Yorb, I multitask, quickly searching for the nearest electronics store on my phone and, although there's nothing near the main drag of the Las Vegas strip that can provide me with the equipment I need, I find a store out in the desert a few miles that looks as though it will have me covered. I need to get these nanobots out of me before I become too horny to control them yet again.

Yorb is nowhere to be found, and for a moment I'm ready to give up, thinking that he's left the casino completely, but as I'm about to head out onto the strip looking for him I suddenly catch a glimpse of the dinosaur's familiar face over at the blackjack table. He doesn't look happy.

I step up to the table and Yorb sees me, but immediately averts his eyes, looking down at the green felt as I watch. I have no idea how many chips he might have started with, but from the looks of it he's not doing so hot.

The dealer shows a ten of hearts, and then motions to Yorb. Yorb's cards total thirteen, which is not a terribly good position to be in. Yorb hits, and he receives another card, which pushes his total up above twenty-one. A loss.

The dealer takes Yorb's bet away, leaving him with an even smaller stack of chips as he shakes his head in disgust.

"Hey, can I talk to you?" I ask Yorb.

He looks at me for a moment, but ignores my concern, immediately turning his attention back to the game. There's something horribly vacant about Yorb's movements, as if he's just going through the motions in an effort to simply give his money away.

Yorb pushes his entire stack out onto the table with one claw, betting it all.

"How much is that?" I ask.

Yorb ignores me, but when he's not looking an older woman at the table turns to me and whispers, "Twelve grand."

"Oh my god." I gasp, trying to cover my mouth and hide my reaction. If that's all he's got left, then I'm terrified to find out how much Yorb started with.

A new set of cards is dealt, with Yorb once again ending up on a total of thirteen. My heart is thundering in my chest now, and I want desperately to pull him away from the table but I know that the hand has already started and, at this point, there's nothing I can do about it.

"Hit." Yorb tells the dealer.

Another card comes down and I breathe a sigh of relief. It's a six of hearts, totaling nineteen, a perfectly respectable place to stand in blackjack.

Yorb however, has other plans. "Hit." He says again.

Even the dealer gives him a strange look, knowing full well that the chances of this turning out well are slim to none. I'm not much for statistics, but I'm knowledgeable enough to know that this is a bad play. There are only eight cards in the entire desk that can keep Yorb from going over twenty-one and losing everything. Reluctantly, the dealer lays down yet another card for Yorb.

It's a two.

The entire table bursts into a cheer, completely blown away by this bold, yet incredibly stupid, play that has somehow worked out in the stegosaurus's favor. I clap my hands together loudly, relieved.

Yorb, however, doesn't move, hardly noticing that another card has even been given to him. His eyes lowered, Yorb simply waits for the cheering and excitement to die down and then finally says, one final time. "Hit me."

The dealer looks confused. "Sir, you have twenty one."

Yorb nods. "I understand."

I shake my head in utter confusion, helpless to do anything as the self-destruction unfolds before me. The entire table is utterly dumbfounded, exchanging glances with one another as the dealer slowly lays down another card, a card whose value is completely inconsequential. Regardless, Yorb will lose.

"Thirty one." The dealer says, a sadness in his voice, then pulls the rest of Yorb's chips towards him.

Immediately, Yorb stands up and leaves the table.

"Hey!" I shout, chasing after him. "What the fuck was that?"

Yorb ignores me, simply stepping around as I attempt to post myself in front of him. He soon arrives at an ATM and inserts his card.

"Jesus, what are you doing?" I ask.

"Getting more cash." Yorb tells me, flatly.

I try desperately to grab his card out of his hands, which finally gets Yorb to at least stop and spin towards me in frustration. I can see now that his eyes are brimming with tears, the anxiety and darkness of his addiction finally catching up with him.

"Oh god." I sigh, and then open my arms for a hug.

Yorb pushes me away. "No."

"Yorb, I'm sorry." I say. "I have no idea who those people were up in the room, I swear."

He laughs to himself. "Oh great." Yorb scoffs, rolling his eyes sarcastically. "That makes everything so much better."

"I'm so sorry." I repeat.

Suddenly, his entire demeanor shifts from a deep self-loathing to sharp anger. "Are you kidding me? We came here together, to help each other get better. It was stupid of me to think that we could have connected this quickly with you, it was stupid of me to believe in love."

I shake my head. "It's not what you think."

"Then what is it?" Yorb shouts. "We're both addicts, I get it, we're sick, but I'm not sick enough to do that kind of shit to you."

"I'm not either!" I protest.

"What does that even mean?" Yorb asks. "What are you saying?"

I pause for a moment, trying my best to figure out how to reveal my secret.

"I think I need to show you, not tell you." I explain. "Otherwise, you're not going to believe me."

Yorb throws his hands up. "Then show me!"

Suddenly, right then and there, I transform into a helicopter.

Yorb's visceral mood immediately shifts into a state of fear and wonder, his mouth hanging open as he stares at my new form.

"How?" Is all that he can say, reaching out and touching me lightly on the windshield.

"It's a long story." I tell him.

Yorb glances around to see if anyone else has noticed this miracle unfolding before his very eyes, but everyone else is completely preoccupied by the flashing lights that hum and dance across the screens before them. The last thing they are worried about is a handsome helicopter.

"I don't understand." Yorb stammers. "Please, try to explain."

"There was an accident at work." I tell him.

"What kind of accident?"

I let out a long sigh, unsure of how to lay all of this out, and then finally flip into computer scientist mode. "I was exposed to a highly advanced nanobot swarm. It's programmed to lock onto my entire molecular structure and, within reason, give me the ability to transform into a helicopter."

"Within reason." Yorb repeats back to me, with a laugh.

"Do you understand what I'm telling you?" I ask.

Yorb shakes his head. "I have no idea, but it's blowing my mind."

We stand for a moment like this, Yorb still reeling from my admission while I prepare myself for the inevitable fallout from the next one. I feel an anxious tingling across my entire body.

I notice now that Yorb is practically shaking with rage. "So you've been Chibs this whole time?"

I sigh. "Yes, but it's not my fault. It's like Chibs is taking over now, trying to control me, trying to break free."

"How could you do this to me?" The dinosaur stammers. "You're the reason that I relapsed. You tricked me."

"I know." I say. "It was…"

I let the words trail off, unable to entirely sum up the horror that I've inflicted on this man who's been nothing but incredible to me.

"I'm sorry." I repeat. "I should've never let him get so out of control."

I immediately transform back into my normal self.

Yorb just shakes his head, still reeling from surreal bomb that I've dropped. "I think you should go back to Los Angeles." He finally says.

"What?" I stammer.

"You're not safe for me to be around." Yorb says. "I don't understand any of this stuff about Chibs taking over, I don't know what it's like to have some other person inside me trying to get out, either. I can't help you anymore. I tried that already and look what happened."

"But you do know what it's like to have another person inside of you!" I protest. "You're an addict."

Frustrated, Yorb simply throws his claws up in the air and turns to walk away. "I'll have the front desk order you a rental car." He calls back over his shoulder. "I don't ever want to see you again."

And then suddenly, just like that, he's gone, disappearing into the milling crowd of gamblers on the casino floor.

11 ESCAPE FROM THE KEEN DANGLER

I feel as though the wind has been knocked out of me, my soul completely deflated as I stand here surrounded by people, yet completely alone. If I hadn't just moments before satiated my powerful sexual desires, then I would assuredly be spinning into yet another session of vapid lustful fucking. Instead, I feel nothing but an overwhelming sadness.

After standing here in silence for some unknown amount of time, I notice a group of large men in security uniforms walking directly towards me.

"Sir?" The largest of the bunch asks as he approaches. "Are you Mr. John Hams?"

I nod, still in a daze from the devastating loss of Yorb, the image of this incredible dinosaur walking right out of my life just repeating over and over again in my head.

"Could you come with us please?" The man asks.

Snapping out of it, I size the men up and immediately realize that running is no use, they are massive and carry tasers strapped to their belts. I nod again, and soon the group of us is crossing the casino floor towards an unmarked door, two of the guards behind me and two in the front. I'm vaguely aware of the strangeness that they know my name, given the fact that I checked in under Yorb's reservation, but I'm too defeated at the moment to care.

The exit leads to a stretch of white walled hallway that we continue down until reaching a second door, which is opened for me. The men do not follow me inside, but instead motion towards a chair in the middle of an otherwise empty room for me to sit at. The walls are cement, save for one, which appears to be one-way glass.

"Have a seat, John." One of the large men says. "The pit boss will be in shortly to speak with you."

I nod and take a seat in the chair as the men leave, locking the door behind them. It's only now that I realize how much trouble I might be in, but without knowing exactly what kind, or why, I still somehow refrain from panicking. My senses are numb with heartbreak.

It's not long before the door opens up and a man steps inside, his face long and fearsome and his eyes set deep like dark, black pools.

"Hello, John." He says. "Thank you for your cooperation."

I smile as pleasantly as I can. "Of course."

"I'm Randall Torrance, the pit boss here at The Keen Dangler casino." The man explains, standing before me menacingly as I look up from my seat in the chair. "It looks like you've been enjoying your stay."

"How do you mean?" I ask.

"Well, we have camera's everywhere. You know this, right?" He counters.

"So?"

"First of all, we don't allow that kind of activity in our restrooms." Randall tells me with a slight scoff. "But, what really caught my eye was the... helicopter shape shifting."

I try to play dumb and give him an awkward laugh, "What?"

"Listen, we have everything on high definition video." Randall tells me. "I watched it myself about ten times before we approached you, but it's there."

My heart is now pounding out of my chest and I'm kicking myself for letting this get so out of control. It was one thing for my secret to be contained, but now it's getting out into the world and, at this point, the consequences are beyond prediction. There's no stopping it now.

"Are you aware that you're wanted by the FBI?" Randall asks me.

I shake my head. "No, what for?"

Randall pulls a sheet of paper out of the inside pocket of his finely tailored jacket and unfolds it, reading aloud. "Theft of government property and treason."

"Shit." I instinctively mumble aloud, realizing what this means.

Detectives Kellogg and Peek have gone back over the footage from

Buttcorp and confirmed that I was lying, and now I've become a threat to national security.

"According to the information that we've gathered, it would appear that you've pissed off somebody at Buttcorp enough to get the feds involved." Randall tells me, confirming my suspicions. "You took your Vegas vacation at the right time but, unfortunately, changing shape like that isn't a good way of laying low."

"Please." I counter. "You don't understand, it's not my fault."

Randall smirks. "Who's fault it is is none of my business." He tells me. "Keeping this casino running is my business and, despite my fascination with your apparent ability, criminals like yourself are not welcome here. There's no telling how much havok you could cause if you were to spin that rotor on the casino floor."

"But you allow other living objects!" I counter. "I've seen living helicopters in here! Living jet planes!"

"But you're a human." The man interjects angrily. "A shifter. An abomination. The police are on their way."

Stung by true discrimination for the first time, I start to protest, to beg him for my release, but at this point I'm not even sure if it matters anymore. Maybe a cold hard cell is exactly what I need, having lost control of myself to the point where I'm hurting those closest to me, extinguishing the potential for love before it even starts. I'm exhausted, tired of running and hiding.

"Okay." I finally say. "That's probably for the best."

Randall nods. "Good."

It takes only a few seconds for my leg to start shaking, trembling as though an earthquake is coursing through the chair below me. I reach down and try to hold myself still but before I know it the strange sensation is pulsing through my arm and then suddenly my entire body is trembling. Unsure of what's happening I look back over my shoulder at the one way glass behind me, which shows off my distorted and shifting face in its reflection.

My transition between personalities is no longer within my control.

"Oh fuck," I manage to stammer.

The next thing I know, I'm transforming into a massive, handsome helicopter, my blades breaking free from the chair below me and smashing it to pieces.

Randall is completely awestruck by both my incredible transformation and my equally incredible body. His mouth hangs agape, eyes firmly drawn down towards my ripped abs.

"You gonna keep staring like that or are you gonna be a man and touch them?" I ask in a voice that's not my own.

Randall looks conflicted, a professional torn between his job and his hardwired sexual compulsion for nice abs.

Trapped within the body of Chibs Pratt, I suddenly realize that if I don't defend myself against capture then he will. We share one another's cellular structure, taking turns as we rent out the being that was once solely my own, but with sharing comes a commitment to preservation. At least, until I can find a means of shutting him down for good.

"Stop this." Randall says, slowly and carefully, as if forcing the words from his mouth.

Chibs lets his massive, engorged cock hang down from the bottom of his hull. "You don't like me?" He coos.

Randall shakes his head. "Stop."

Chibs beckons towards Randall with a blade, coaxing the man to come closer and closer. Sure enough, even he is unable to resist the charms of such a perfectly shaped aircraft.

The man takes two steps towards us as we tilt back on our boom tail, exposing ourselves to him completely.

"Would you like to give it a suck?" Chibs asks.

Unable to resist such an incredible helicopter cock, Randall nods and climbs down to the floor, now crawling towards us on his hands and knees. Chibs places our blades on the back of his head and begins to pump Randall onto our throbbing dick when suddenly, he uses all of his force to propel him down onto the floor with a loud crack.

Randall immediately collapses onto the ground before us with a broken nose, or worse, completely unconscious as a small pool of blood starts to bloom across the concrete floor around him. We tilt back up and Chibs looks directly at us in the reflection of the one way glass, then says to me, "Alright, I took care of the dirty work, now you get us out of here."

Suddenly, I'm trembling again, unable to stop the transformation as I swiftly turn back into myself.

Almost immediately, I can hear shouting from behind the glass. Knowing that I only have a few seconds to react, I make a break for the door and then burst out into the long white hallway.

I wasn't paying nearly enough attention coming in, so my first and most important question is to determine which way leads out. Looking up and down the hallway, it's almost impossible to say, each of them appearing to me seemingly endless stretches of sterile corridor.

"John Hams!" I suddenly hear familiar voice shouting.

I turn to see Yorb waving me towards him down the hallway to my left, while a group of security guards come barreling out of a doorway to my right.

I take off running towards the beautiful stegosaurus, who waits until I reach him and then begins to sprint along beside me as we make our way through the maze. Fortunately, he seems to know exactly where he's going.

The next thing I know, we are plowing through an exit door that leads to an alleyway behind the casino, where Yorb's car is waiting in what is surely not a legal space. We jump inside just as the security guards exit the casino behind us, but by the time they've reached the street we are already flying out across the asphalt at blinding speeds, Yorb's low riding vehicle tearing around the corner with a loud roar.

Moments later, we're several blocks away, panting loudly as Yorb and me catch our breath.

"Thank you." I say, hardly able to get the words out. "Oh my god, thank you so much, Yorb."

Yorb is still brooding, his eyes focused directly ahead through the windshield. "You're welcome."

"How'd you know where to find me?" I ask.

"I saw them take you away." He explains. "And I followed them. Besides, the guts of these giant casinos are all pretty much the same, and I've seen my share of back rooms." The light at our intersection turns green, but Yorb doesn't go anywhere. "Where to now?"

I'm suddenly hit with a moment of panic. "Do you have our stuff? Is my laptop in here?"

Yorb nods. "I went up and grabbed it all from the room."

I'm so happy to hear this that I reach out across the center console and wrap my arms around Yorb, hugging him tight and giving him a kiss on the cheek.

He tries not to react, still upset with me, but I see the slightest hint of a smile flare up at the corner of his dinosaur lips. A car honks behind us.

"Where to?" Yorb repeats. "You destroyed my Vegas detox, so now it's your call where we go to fix all of this."

I pull out my phone and read aloud an address the cars navigation system. "1820 Desert Inn Rd."

The cars computer whirs to life, calculating the fastest path to get us there.

"1820 Desert Inn Rd." The car's computer voice announces. "Buck Trungle's Electronics."

Yorb glances over at me as he takes off across the intersection. "You've got a lot of explaining to do, Helicopter Man." He says.

The best thing about a guy who's seen the world, like Yorb, is that he's open to new ideas, even if those ideas sound utterly insane at first. This couldn't be more apparent than when I finished explaining to him the way I'd been trapped in a chamber and, unwillingly, been exposed to these nanobots, giving life to a repressed and destructive side of my personality named Chibs Pratt.

I suppose it's easier after you see someone change into a helicopter right before your very eyes, but what is even more astonishing than his belief is his forgiveness; Forgiveness for lying, forgiveness for destroying his prior relationship, and forgiveness for dragging him into this mess.

Of course, true unconditional forgiveness is hard, but it's a little easier when you have a split personality to blame. Even *I* can't be sure how much of these digressions were Chibs and how much of them were caused by my own sick jealousy.

Yorb and I do agree on one thing, however. That Chibs Pratt needs to be shut down for good, before he hurts anyone else or causes me to be relegated to the inside of a test tube for the rest of my life.

As we fly through the desert I sit in the passenger seat of Yorb's powerful sports car, programming away at my laptop as we close in on our destination.

"So you think you can hack into the nanobots without all of your equipment from the lab?" Yorb questions, the third time that he's asked me this already.

"Hopefully," I admit. "I mean, the hard part is getting them in there, controlling them is fairly easy, actually, because they are programmed to listen to the commands in my own brain."

"So why can't you just tell them to shut down yourself?" Yorb asks.

"In a effort to keep the nanobot program from corrupting, which was a huge hurdle for us in the lab, we started coding in a self preservation algorithm." I explain. "In other words, once the program has entered its host, it's going to do everything that it can to stay alive."

"Like artificial intelligence?" Yorb asks.

"In a limited form, yes, although not enough for the program to become self aware." I say. "It cannot take control of the host."

Yorb flashes me a skeptical look and I immediately realize what I've said.

"Looks like you should have kept things little more limited." Yorb tells me.

I nod. "Yeah, we should have." In some ways I like this theory, that the terrible things I've been doing as Chibs were actually products of intelligence within the program itself, and not a desperate explosion of my own pent up helicopter subconscious.

I feel a tiny bit of guilt lifted up off of my shoulders, but only slightly.

"So what do you need from this computer store?" Yorb asks.

"Simple stuff, really." I say. "Most of what I need is already right here as software on this computer. Other than that, it's just going to take a router, a large external hard drive and a few specialty cables that will hopefully be in stock."

"Sounds good." Yorb says, nodding. He looks over at me, the anger and disappointment finally fading from his yellow eyes as I glance up from my computer screen and meet his gaze. "You're gonna be okay." The dinosaur tells me.

His assurance hits me right in the heart, warming me to the core in a time when I need it the most. Unfortunately, all I can think to say in response is, "I'm sorry."

Yorb nods in understanding, then pulls out his coin with on hand and shoves it into its special slot in the dashboard. "Don't mention it." He responds.

I spot a small, desolate building coming into view in the distance. It looks as though it was once a gas station, now converted into a small, strange computer workshop on the edge of the Las Vegas county line. There's nothing else for miles but open road and empty stretches of golden desert sand.

"There it is!" I shout excitedly.

We pull into the dusty parking lot and jump out immediately, jogging over to the front doors and ripping them open. A bell jingles loudly above my head as we step inside, apparently the only customers that have been on the premises in quite a while.

"Hello?" I call out, making my way deeper and deeper into the hallways cluttered with all kinds of strange, miscellaneous computer equipment.

There's a bit of shuffling from the back room and then suddenly a totally ripped, gray haired man emerges, pushing his thick rimmed glasses up onto his nose.

"Buck Trungle?" I ask.

"Can I help you?" Comes his response, slightly bewildered by my excitement at his odd little shop.

"Yes." I smile. "Handing him a list of parts that I'll be needing."

Buck Trungle nods. "I think we've got what you're looking for."

12 BUCK TRUNGLE'S ELECTRONICS

Buck has generously allowed me to spend most of the day programming out back, in a small fenced off portion of the shop that sits outside, open to the warm desert air but shaded by a small roof above. Out here, there are plenty of places to plug in and get to work, and after Yorb greases him with a rather substantial hourly rate to let us toil here unhindered, Buck seems to be much more of a happy man than a crazy one.

There is something strange about that man that I can't quite put my finger on, something familiar and welcoming. The shop itself is quite unusual, covered in framed posters of blown up science fiction and romance novel covers, yet I feel perfectly at home here. Buck explains that he used to be a writer, but after several lawsuits involving his own books, the man finally decided to get into a different line of work. Rejecting society, he drove out here to the desert and began working on an idea that he had for a universe collapsing button, whatever that means.

I'm one of the most brilliant scientists that there is, and I still have no idea what Buck is talking about. Unfortunately, when I question the man's progress towards the creation of his button, expressing my cautious doubt and gentle criticism, the aging scientist dismisses me completely, claiming that he has already created the button in other universes and that this one is still trying to catch up.

He explains that there are many level of the universe all existing at the same time, past, present and future all at once. He explains that we are all creations of an author named Chuck Tingle who exist in a fictional world. He explains that, depending on how many times the button has been

90

pressed, having sex with a dinosaur could be seen as utterly absurd, which I find to be slightly offensive.

Long story short, Buck Trungle is crazy.

Despite working as fast as I can to hack into the nanobot program, it's sunset by the time I start making real progress. I created most of this code myself, from the ground up, so getting in there and messing around with it is as simple as I had expected, my only hindrance being the slightly dated amalgamation of equipment that I'm working with. Still, it gets the job done, and soon enough I find myself booting up all the gear for my first trial run, just as the sun begins to blossom purple over the distant mountain ranges.

"Yorb!" I shout, calling the stegosaurus over from his seat across the patio, where he's been deep in thought as he watches me work.

Yorb stands up and walks over, curiously looking at the laptop screen before me, even though he has no idea what any of the scrolling lines of code mean.

"I think I'm ready." I tell him. "I think this is it."

Yorb can tell that there's something strange in the way that I say this. "What is it?" He asks, immediately cutting to the chase. "What's wrong?"

"Nothing." I tell him, shaking my head and lying poorly despite my best efforts.

"Something's wrong, and I know it." Yorb says, his intuition serving him well. "Tell me what's happening."

"Well," I offer, cautiously. "I'm about to confirm the edit that I've just finished on the nanobot script, but I'm not exactly sure what's going to happen to me when I do it."

"What do you mean? I thought you were just going to shut off all the little... robots." Yorb questions.

"I am." I explain. "But they're part of my cellular structure now, they'll always be there. My edit here will hopefully disable any of their shape changing functions, but there's also the very strong chance that the nanobots will just shut off entirely."

"What do you mean shut off enitrely?" Yorb demands to know, his unease completely showing through now. "Is that dangerous?"

I hesitate for a moment, not wanting to tell him but quickly realizing that it's the only fair thing to do. "Meaning that when I press enter on this keyboard I could be killed instantly."

Yorb closes his eyes, not wanting to deal with the severity of this situation but also realizing, to his credit, that there are really no other options. If I don't' do this then I'll cease to exist anyway, completely consumed by the personality of Chibs Pratt. "John." Is all that Yorb can manage to say, a dinosaur tear rolling down his cheek, "I don't want you to get hurt."

"I know." I tell him, "I'm so sorry, but this is the only way."

Yorb takes me into his muscular retile arms and holds me tight, his cool touch putting me immediately at ease. There's a magic that moves between us, one that I first recognized that night we spent together at the diner, but I now know had been there all along since the very beginning.

Our embrace seems to last a lifetime, but when Yorb finally pulls away he stops and looks deep into my eyes, which are also now beginning to fill with tears despite my best efforts.

"I think…" I stammer, the words within me bubbling ferociously to the surface of my soul, where they can no longer be contained. "I think I love you."

Yorb kisses me deeply, then pulls back. "I love you, too." He says. "I love you, John Hams."

The second that my name leaves Yorb's lips I can feel something surge within me, a strange and powerful sensation that covers my body in a trembling, quaking ache.

"Oh fuck." I say aloud, my voice cracking as it morphs into that of Chibs Pratt. "He's trying to stop me."

I suddenly find myself sinking deeper and deeper into the shell of my own body, unable to control the movements of the beautiful, helicopter straightjacket that forms around my being. I try to will the cells within me to stop and revert back to their original state, but it's no use. I've lost all control.

I see Yorb look down at the laptop that sits just beyond his grasp, immediately recognizing what he has to do, for better or worse. Without hesitation, Yorb reaches across me and goes for the space bar, but my own powerful helicopter blade reaches out abruptly to stop him.

"Don't even try it." Chibs says.

Suddenly, Chibs' blade is grabbing Yorb by the throat, solidly clamped onto his neck with a tight, vice like grip. His arm is extending upward, stretching farther and farther as the swarming nanobots create an ever-lengthening limb. The dinosaur tries his best to claw Chibs off of him, but it's no use, the strength of his nanobot infused cells is too powerful.

From deep within Chibs Pratt's mind I'm screaming for him to stop, but my monstrous mechanical creation is in no mood to listen.

Yorb's face is becoming paler as he hangs from Chibs's grasp, struggling for air.

"You're very sexy." Chibs says, looking sadly at Yorb. "And I like you a lot, but I feel like we're outgrown each other."

Yorb tries to respond, his feet kicking the air wildly just a few inches off of the ground, but he doesn't have enough air in his lungs to form the words.

"It's not you." Chibs explains. "It's me. I just can't be around someone who's going to try and shut me down like this. That goes for you *and* for John Hams. I'm afraid this is the end of both of you."

From deep within Chibs, I begin to cry, but no physical tears fall from my eyes. I'm too far gone now, swallowed up by the handsome helicopter body of Chibs Pratt.

The light of Yorb's soul has nearly gone out, but in his last moments I see a strange expression cross his scaly face, as if remembering something incredibly important. Moments later, I see his claw reach deep into his pocket, scrambling for something hidden deep within the fabric. Yorb pulls out his lucky coin.

As soon as I realize what's about to happen Chibs does as well, but it's already too late. In a final moment of desperation, Yorb throws the coin down at the laptop below him, striking the spacebar with incredible accuracy.

Immediately, a series of coded lines begin to dance across the screen, scrolling at blinding speeds as the computer's internal processor whirs to life.

I'm suddenly hit with an intense pain, every nerve in my body flaring up at once. Chibs drops Yorb and rocks back and forth on his skids, struggling to find any kind of solace from the searing discomfort. His senses are my senses, and together the helicopter and me writhe on the ground in agony.

My thoughts are flooded with distant memories of my childhood and then my teenage years, all the way up until now, at this very moment. It all happens in a flash but everything is there, from the beginning to the end, every choice that has lead me to this terrible place.

Then, however, I remember Yorb.

Soon his gorgeous stegosaurus face is coming towards me through the haze in my brain, smiling sweetly as beams of light shine out from behind him with heavenly grace. The pain immediately begins to fade, replaced by a soft, but pleasant ache.

"I'm sorry." I tell him.

Yorb chuckles. "You don't need to be sorry."

"Am I dead?" I ask.

"Nope." Yorb tells me. "Alive and well." As he says this, the glowing white light around him suddenly dissipates into a purple, sunset laden sky behind.

I'm lying on my back, still on the patio behind Buck Trungle's shop.

"Whoa." I say, holding my hand up in front of my face. I immediately recognize it as my own. Hesitantly, I make my best attempt to alter it in some way, to flatten the flesh into a long metallic blade. Nothing happens, and I breathe out a sigh of relief.

13 THE HELICOPTER MAN RISES

It's late as Yorb and me cross back through the desert, not making the usual route from east to west, but instead heading due south as fast as we can. Despite handling our biggest problem, Chibs Pratt, we still have plenty of legal troubles to worry about. Until we can get it all sorted, we'll be headed south of the border, at which point Yorb plans on hiring a lawyer who can take care of everything for us. We could always turn ourselves in, but Buttcorp is not a company that will have any kind of mercy on me, nor will the United States government when dealing with the potential exposure of military secrets. This is what my life has somehow become.

Of course, running doesn't really help either of our cases, but then again we've been running since the beginning, caught up in misunderstanding after misunderstanding that has eventually snowballed into this. It feels natural to just keep going; romantic even.

"How do we know that he's gone for good?" Yorb asks me.

"I don't know." I tell him. "It's hard to say, but I certainly don't feel a helicopter inside of me, if that makes any sense."

Our headlights sweep across the desert highway as Yorb turns down the car radio, a sign that our conversation is about to get heavy.

"We're a great team." He says.

I nod in agreement.

"A team needs balance, life needs balance." He continues, almost to himself. "It's not just black and white like I thought that it was."

"I'm beginning to realize that too." I say, staring out the window as the highways center line whips past. "I mean, I think that billionaire dinosaur abstinence was good for me, but it also created a monster."

"It did." Yorb agrees. "Don't get me wrong, I think we should take it slow, maybe even stay in the program a while. Little steps."

"Do they have sexaholic meetings in Mexico?" I ask.

Yorb cracks a smile. "I guess we're gonna find out."

The two of us sit in silence for a moment, along with our own racing thoughts about whatever the future may hold. I let my hand slip across the center console and grab a hold of claw, which elicits that instant chemistry between us.

"We still need to make sure she's gone for good, though." Yorb ads.

At first I'm not completely sure what he's getting at but, the second that I do, I'm filled with a surge of excitement and anxiety. I accidentally squeeze him a little tighter for a moment, then loosen up again.

"There's really only one way to know for sure." I tell the handsome stegosaurus.

Yorb nods. "Then back to celibacy."

"Of course." I tell him.

Almost immediately, Yorb pulls over onto the side of the road and climbs out of the car, leaving the lights on and the engine running. I step out with him, and then moments later we are meeting in front of the car before the wash of golden headlights. Yorb and me embrace each other feverishly, our lips locked in a passionate embrace.

My heart rate elevated, my body trembling, I'm happy to find that there are no signs of Chibs Pratt making any kind of appearance. Of course, the reality of this heated sexual exchange between me and Yorb has much more to do with the fact that we have yet to make love together without the helicopter interrupting, than a legitimate test of Chibs Pratt's assumed demise.

I don't mind. Whatever the reason, I want this billionaire dinosaur and I want him now.

Without another human being for miles on this empty stretch of desert highway, I quickly tear off my shirt and watch gladly as Yorb does the same. His green body is just as incredible as ever, perfect other than the large bandage across his right side. I touch it gently with my hands and then work my way up to his toned, muscular chest.

This is the first time that I've exposed my real self to Yorb, the first time that I've truly revealed my skin to him without the glossy illusion of

Chibs' metallic hull between us. It's a daunting exercise for me, but as we look into one another's eyes I find that there is nothing but trust. Yorb is admiring me, the real me, and regardless of how I feel about myself, I know that he thinks I'm perfect exactly the way that I am; a man, not a helicopter.

Suddenly overwhelmed with passion, I drop to my knees and unbutton Yorb's pants, pulling them down and letting his massive erect cock spring forth. If there was a time for Chibs to show himself, it would be now, but nothing of the sort happens. I'm completely me.

Instead, I open wide and swallow Yorb's shaft deep into my hungry mouth. The gorgeous dinosaur lets out a satisfied moan, leaning back and lifting his head skyward like a howling wolf of the desert.

I move up and down, letting Yorb's stegoshaft slip gracefully between my lips as I pleasure him. With one hand I cradle his hanging balls, and with the other I reach up and take his hand in mine, grasping tightly.

"You're incredible." Yorb moans.

I push down farther and farther until hitting my gag reflex, which had previously been easy to overcome thanks to my nanobot cells. Instead, I find myself stuck, and eventually I'm forced to come up for air in a frantic gasp.

"Are you alright?" Yorb asks.

"Yes." I assure him. "I just need to do this."

"You don't need to do anything." He tells me.

I shake my head. "I need to do this, Yorb."

I center myself and then try again, this time relaxing my throat as much as possible as Yorb's cock slides deeper and deeper into me. His length is incredible, and at first I retch a little as it hits the back of my throat. Moments later, however, I somehow manage to relax enough that Yorb's massive dinosaur dick slides all the way inside. I proudly look up at him and give a playful gay wink, Yorb's shaft entirely consumed as my lips press lightly up against his rock hard abs.

"Fuck." Is all that this amazing beast can manage to get out, overwhelmed by my expert deep throating skills. "That's incredible, John Hams."

The sound of my own name sends a pleasant chill down my spine. This is all that I had wanted all along.

Moments later, I find Yorb pulling me up to my feet with his muscular arms. He kisses me deeply and then pushes me back against the hood of

97

the car, where I lay happily as the beautiful dinosaur removes my jeans and tosses them to the side. My boxer briefs come off next, and suddenly I find myself completely exposed to the warm desert air.

Yorb leans down and immediately gets to sucking my swollen cock with his stegosaurus jaws, which sends all kinds of incredible volts of pleasure throughout my body. I arch my back against the hood as Yorb satisfies my senses.

The dinosaur certainly knows how to give a blowjob, finding no trouble at all with quickly bringing my body dangerously close to cumming. The feeling builds within me in wave after blissful wave, every one becoming more powerful than the last until finally I just can't take it anymore and I force myself to push him back.

"I want to blow this load." I tell him. "But I want to do it with you inside of me."

Yorb smiles and pulls me down the hood slightly so that my muscular ass is hanging right off of the edge. Next, he aligns his rock hard shaft with my aching butthole, his head teasing against my entrance while I beg for him to push it in.

"Fuck me!" I demand.

Yorb stops for a moment. "It's nice to hear you say that in your own voice."

"Fuck." I start, reaching down and grapping him around the waist with one hand. "Me." As I finish repeating the phrase, I pull Yorb forward and his mammoth cock disappears completely inside of me, stretching my taut anus to the brink.

I let out a loud groan, not entirely prepared to take his substantial size within my butthole. I've been doing plenty of fucking lately, but I immediately realize that it has all been within the body of someone else, and that my own ass is still that of a man who's been saving himself for three years.

As I look up at the stars above us, twinkling beautify across the open Nevada sky, I can't think of a better moment to give myself away than this.

Yorb begins to pump in and out of me, slowly but firmly as I tremble at his skilled touch. My muscular legs are spread wide for him, held back as he slams into me at an ever-escalating speed. Soon enough, Yorb is hammering into me with everything he's got, his green hips rattling loudly against the hood of the car.

I reach down and start to beat myself off to the rhythm of the dinosaur's powerful slams.

Once again, I can feel the profound sensation of an impending orgasm blossoming deep within. It grows quickly, spreading out across my body in a series of violent quakes until my entire being is convulsing. There is too much pleasure locked up inside, bubbling over without any place left to go.

"Oh my god." I start to mumble. "Oh my god."

"I love you so much." Yorb tells me, his yellow eyes aflame with truth and passion.

"I love you, too!" I tell him, my legs suddenly kicking out straight. "I'm cumming!"

Yorb doesn't let up for a second as the orgasm surges through me like a lightning bolt, pounding away at my frame with his muscular body. All of the tension from the last few days is suddenly released within me, exploding across every ounce of my being with blinding love. A series of hot semen blasts erupt from the head of my cock, shooting into the air with incredible strength before splattering back down onto me.

I let out a blood-curdling howl that echos out across the desert landscape, cascading across the hills and valleys until it bounces back to us. I'm outside of my body now, looking down at myself as I writhe and spasm on the hood of Yorb's red sportscar.

This is the second time that this dinosaur's sexual prowess has given me an out of body experience, but the first that I've been able to look down and truly see myself without an unfamiliar face staring back at me. I can see tears of joy flowing down my cheeks in beautiful glistening streaks, truly happy within my own skin.

I suddenly realize that Yorb is cumming as well, buckling forward as he ejects several pumps of semen within me. His eyes are clenched tight as he lets out a guttural cry of his own.

The entire experience seems to defy time and space, stretching on and on for what feels like forever until suddenly I'm thrown back into reality, lying in exhaustion on the warm hood of the car with Yorb on top of me, breathing hard.

"That was amazing." I whisper into his ear.

Yorb and I sit at a crowded diner in San Diego, California, just a few miles from Mexico. The food is surprisingly good, a mixture of down home American favorites with a south of the border flair. I'm content, happy that Yorb and me are on the cusp of starting a new life together, one filled with romance and adventure.

I take a big bite of my jalapeño burger, the spicy flavors dancing playfully across my tongue.

Since discovering that Chibs Pratt is no longer lurking somewhere deep within my subconscious, everything seems to have a little more bite, including the food in front of me.

"This is great!" I tell Yorb, who laughs out loud and reaches across the table to wipe a small splatter of catsup from my chin.

"I can tell!" He jokes.

As I sit here chewing, I start to actually wonder if Chibs is truly gone for good. Sure, the nanobots within my body have been deprogrammed and rendered inoperable, but that's not really what made Chibs so powerful in the first place. At the end of the day, it was my own insecurities that gave him the power that he had; two sides of the same unlucky coin.

Chibs Pratt may be gone physically, unable to manifest himself out here in the real world, but I think the helicopter will always be lurking somewhere within me.

I suddenly notice that Yorb is looking past me, over my shoulder towards the door of the restaurant. He is frozen in a strange state of fear and confusion, his burger held with utter stillness halfway between his plate and his mouth.

I turn in my chair to follow his gaze and then freeze as well, unable to process the sight that greets me, defying all sense and reason.

There, in the doorway of the restaurant, stands Chibs Pratt; not in any sort of metaphorical or whimsical way, but the helicopter himself.

Chibs looks directly at me and our gazes immediately lock.

"Is that..." Yorb asks, trailing off as his brain answers his own utterly impossible question.

"Oh my god." Is all that I can manage to respond.

Chibs begins to cross through the restaurant towards us, sauntering back and forth on his skids until he reaches the table and stops, looking down at us with his massive helicopter eyes.

"I'm sorry." The vehicle finally says.

"What?" Is all that I can respond, completely blown away by the sight of this aircraft that once only existed in my subconscious mind.

"I'm sorry." Chibs repeats. "My self preservation programming was a little out of line back there."

"And now?" I ask, my heart pounding hard in my chest.

"Buck reactivated me." Explains the helicopter. "With some minor adjustments."

I exchange glances with Yorb.

"Can we talk about this somewhere a little more private?" The helicopter continues as the restaurant hustles and bustles around us.

Out behind the diner, the San Diego palms sway back and forth in the cool ocean breeze. Everything here is fresh and new, a welcome break from the desert that remains several hundred miles behind us.

"I need to show you something." Says the helicopter, a holographic video suddenly projected out from his body into the air before Yorb and me. It's a clip from a newsreel, showing my face above the words 'wanted.' There is footage of our exploits at the casino; caught red handed.

It looks as though me and Yorb are more sought after than we thought.

"They know you're headed for the border." The helicopter explains. "You won't make it into Mexico."

I don't even try to protest because, with our faces plastered all over the news, I know that Yorb is right. This plan was doomed to begin with.

"We can turn around, head out East somewhere." My dinosaur lover offers in desperation.

"For how long?" Chibs questions. "You can't just keep running forever."

"He's right." I add. "I can't believe that I'm saying this, but the helicopter is right."

"If you drive anywhere, they'll find you." Chibs Pratt says. "The search is tightening closer and closer every day and they've got a read on Yorb's car."

I let out a long sigh. "So what do we do?"

The helicopter smiles. "Join with me again."

Immediately, I shake my head in vehement opposition. "Oh no, not that again!"

"I'm not the same Chopper anymore." The helicopter proclaims in a smooth, assuring tone. "You'll have full control."

"And why should I trust you?" I ask.

"Because you don't have many more options." Chibs tells me. "It's just as hard for me as it is for you. Once we are joined together with Buck's new programming, I'll be gone forever, just another part of your personality."

The choppers sincerity is stunning and hard to dismiss as just some kind of devious self-preservation tactic. He's right, at this point we don't have many more options.

"Why does Buck want to help us?" I finally ask.

"Thanks to some of the technology you left behind at the shop, he's been able to determine that this particular subset of the Tingleverse is for superheroes. He believes that you're one of them."

"Tingleverse?" I ask. "Superheroes?"

"Yes." The helicopter replies with a nod.

"But I'm just a regular guy, I'm no superhero." I stammer.

"Right now you're not." Explains Chibs. "And right now I'm just a talking helicopter, but together we are Helicopter Man."

Suddenly, from far off in the distance I can hear the faint sound of police sirens, their droning wail slowly drawing closer and closer. Someone in the restaurant must have tipped them off.

"Buck Trungle needs your help." Says Chibs. "The origin story is finished, which means the villains are coming soon."

"Villains?" I ask.

"From the other Tingleverses." Continues the helicopter.

Now the sirens are blaring loud in my ears, emanating from just around the corner.

Finally, I take action, stepping forward and wrapping my arms tightly around the cockpit of the chopper. Almost immediately I can feel myself sliding into the metal, the cells of my body combining with the nanobots once again. I can already tell that there have been some adjustments to the code, however, and the process is quite painless; pleasant even.

I realize now that the chopper half of my personality has been severely upgraded with an Internet connection, a projection screen and an assortment of state of the art weaponry.

"Get in!" I shout to Yorb, once Chibs and me are fused completely.

The stegosaurus does as he's told, throwing open the cockpit door and climbing inside just as the police cruisers round the corner. Several uniformed officers spring out of their vehicles and raise their weapons, but before they can get out a shot I eject a wide net from my front and cover them in a thick, metallic mesh. Before the cops have a chance to recover I'm gone, floating off into the sky with Yorb sitting happily in the passenger seat.

"Where to now, Chibs?" I ask myself.

There's no answer.

"He's gone." Yorb says solemnly, looking out over the beautiful ocean that stretches out below us. "He's inside of you now. Right where he started as just another part of your personality."

I don't even know what to say, suddenly truly realizing the incredible sacrifice that this nanobot swarm has made.

"So where do we go now, Helicopter Man?" Asks Yorb.

I think for a minute, then swerve off and start heading northeast. "Let's go talk to Buck." I tell him confidently. "I've got some super villains to prepare for."

After that, Yorb and me sit in silence for a while, taking in the beautiful desert vistas that quickly begin to extend out before us. We wallow in the presence of one another, and in the peaceful warmth of our mutual love.

There's only one thing that could make this moment even more perfect.

"You know, in all this time, you've been the who pounds my ass." I tell the stegosaurs. "I still haven't gotten a chance to pound yours."

Yorb grins. "Oh yeah? What's stopping you?"

"I've made a commitment." I explain. "I'm only going to pound a dinosaur billionaire's ass if it has a real, deep meaning."

"And you don't feel that with me?" The stegosaurus questions.

"Take off your pants." I instruct, which Yorb does gladly.

"Now what?" Yorb asks.

"Now you better buckle up." I tell him. "Because you're in for a bumpy ride back to Vegas."

Immediately, I adjust my molecular structure and create a massive, thick cock that propels upward from the seat beneath Yorb. My dinosaur lover lets out a yelp of shock and pleasure as my helicopter dick enters him.

"Oh fuck!" Yorb moans. "That feels so fucking good!"

I begin to pump in and out of him at a steady pace, thoroughly enjoying the sensation of penetrating his incredible dinosaurs tightness.

"You're my hero, Helicopter Man." Yorb cries out. "I love you."

A smile crosses my face. I finally feel like a hero, I finally fell like myself.

ABOUT THE AUTHOR

Dr. Chuck Tingle is an erotic author and Tae Kwon Do grandmaster (almost black belt) from Billings, Montana. After receiving his PhD at DeVry University in holistic massage, Chuck found himself fascinated by all things sensual, leading to his creation of the "tingler", a story so blissfully erotic that it cannot be experienced without eliciting a sharp tingle down the spine. Chuck's hobbies include backpacking, checkers and sport.